Tales of the Alhambra for children

Washington Irving

Adapted by Miguel Ángel González

Translation by Diana L. Kelham

Ilustrations by Enrique Bonet Vera

| Coordinación editorial: | José Antonio García Sánchez |
| Diseño: | Francisco José Requena López |

© de la adaptación literaria:	Miguel Ángel González
© de las ilustraciones:	Enrique Bonet Vera
© de las fotografías:	Pablo López Ramírez
© de esta edición:	Editorial Comares
	Polígono Juncaril, parcela 208, 18220, Albolote (Granada)

ISBN: 84-8444-223-3
Depósito Legal: GR-1.679/2000
Impresión y encuadernación: Comares S.L.

Index

Prologue

Washington Irving, the American writer from New York, spent several months in Granada in 1829, actually staying in the palace of the Alhambra. At that time the wonderful Arab building, now a protected historical monument, was inhabited by a variety of popular characters with whom Irving lived and became friends. The tales and traditions that he heard from them, together with a selection of other information, as well as his own very romantic imagination, served as the basis for him to write the Tales of the Alhambra.

His book is a mixture of travellers' tales, anecdotes, personal diary, descriptions and history of local traditions. However, even more important than this, there are seven legends in which magic and imagination shine with special intensity, and which form the "real heart" of the book. They are tales which tell stories of adventure, emotion, mystery and fun, where illusion and reality are intertwined, and at the same time there is a mixture of fantasy and everyday life, past and present. Through these stories, we step into incredible, enchanted chambers, we form part of the group telling tales of horror around a bonfire, we take part in the neighbours' dance in the valley of the Darro, or we contemplate the imaginary court of Boabdil, spellbound beneath the mountain. We are introduced to the proud legendary monarch, the contemptible, greedy mayor, the powerful magician and the modest gardener, the innocent maiden and the enchanted Christian prisoner.

The main scene of action is always the Alhambra; the unique beauty of this monument has the added fascination of becoming a world of mysterious treasures hidden by spells, spirits appearing out of fountains at midnight, phantoms of lovelorn princesses lamenting their misfortune in moonlit towers, ghostly soldiers on guard through the centuries, or monsters such as the headless horse hurling itself at a diabolical gallop through dark avenues on the stroke of midnight.

We have chosen these seven tales for the book, since they will certainly be the most attractive for young readers. The literary adaptation of the original text makes it lighter with the intention of making it more appropriate for our readers, while at the same time we have respected the style and kept most of the nuances that give it personality. As a result of teamwork, drawings and photographs complement the writing and enhance the most significant moments of each of the tales in the places where Washington Irving imagined them, the actual places where his characters lived and which we the readers are lucky enough to relive today.

M.A.G.

Tales of the Alhambra
for children

The Arabian Astrologer

The Gate of Justice

The Arabian Astrologer

Many centuries ago, there was a Moorish king called Aben Habuz who ruled in Granada. He was a retired conqueror who had led a life of robbery and persecution in his youth, but now he was tired and wanted nothing more than peace and quiet to administer the riches he had won and to enjoy to the full the treasures robbed from his neighbours.

However, he had to face younger rivals who were ready to reclaim what he had stolen from their parents. In fact, there were areas of his own territories, previously governed with a rule of iron by this king, where they were ready to take up arms against the old, ill king, and they even threatened to make him prisoner in his own capital. So, he had enemies everywhere, and as Granada is surrounded by high mountains that hide any approaching enemy, Aben Habuz lived in a constant state of vigilance, without knowing where they would attack.

He had towers set up on the mountains and guards along the paths, to no avail, and ordered fires to be lit at night or smoke signals by day if the enemies approached, because they used to appear along some forgotten pass, destroy his possessions and make off with the booty and the prisoners.

Aben Habuz was troubled by these worries, when an ancient Arabian doctor arrived at his court. He had a beard which was as white as snow and reached down to his waist, and he seemed very aged; however, he had come almost the whole way from Egypt on foot, with only the aid of his stick, which was covered in hieroglyphics. His name was Ibrahim Abu Ayub. He was said to have lived at the time of Mahomet and to have spent many years in Egypt, studying the magic of the priests.

It was also said that he had discovered the secret of prolonging life, and that he was more than two centuries old, but as he had discovered this when he was already quite old, he had remained grey-haired and wrinkled.

The old man received a good welcome from the

king, who like most monarchs with many years on their shoulders, began to pay a lot of attention to doctors. He tried to offer him an apartment in his palace, but the astrologer preferred a cave on the hillside high above Granada, where the Alhambra was later built. He had the cave widened to make a spacious hall, with a hole in the roof through which he could gaze at the sky and the stars. He covered the walls with Egyptian symbols and hieroglyphics and with the figures that form the stars, and decorated the hall with objects whose hidden properties were known by him only.

In a very short time the wise man Ibrahim became the king's closest counsellor, consulted by him about any difficulty. One day Aben Habuz complained about the injustice of his neighbours and the continuous vigilance he had to keep in order to protect himself against them. The astrologer said to him:

−Oh my king! In Egypt I saw a wonderful invention of an ancient pagan priest. On a mountain in the city of Borsa there was the bronze figure of a ram, and higher up the figure of a cock, both of which rotated on their axis. Every time there was a threat of an invasion, the ram turned in the direction of the danger and the cock crowed. This was how they warned the city of danger and where it was coming from, so the inhabitants could prepare to defend themselves against it.

–The Lord is great! –exclaimed the pacific Aben Habuz–. I wish I had a magical invention like that. How calmly I would dream with guards like that in the tower!

The astrologer waited for the king to calm down and then continued:

–One day I was sitting on the banks of the Nile, talking to an ancient priest, and he showed me the pyramids which rise up in the desert and he said: "In the centre of the pyramid which you see, in the middle there is the mummy of a great priest, and together with it the wonderful Book of Knowledge, which belonged to King Solomon and which contains all the secrets of magic and art". On hearing these words, my heart burned with the desire to possess that book. With the help of many soldiers and some of the native Egyptians, I opened up a hole in the mass of the pyramid as far as an inner passageway, followed a complicated labyrinth and reached where the mummy of the great priest lay; finally I found the precious book lying on his chest.

–But how can Solomon's Book of Knowledge be of any help to me? –asked Aben Habuz.

—By studying it I have learnt all the magical arts and I can build a talisman such as the talisman of Borsa, and one with greater powers —replied Ibrahim.

—Give me that safeguard, and all my wealth will be at your disposal —begged Aben Habuz.

The astrologer immediately set to work. He had a great tower built on the highest part of the royal palace on the Albayzín hill. In the upper part there was a circular hall, with windows looking towards all four points of the compass, and in front of each of them, on a table with a type of chessboard, there was a tiny wooden army with the figure of the reigning monarch. On each table there was a lance as small as a needle. The hall was permanently closed and the key remained in the king's possession.

On the top of the tower was the bronze statue of a Moorish horseman, with his shield and lance poised in a perpendicular position. His face looked towards the city, but if any enemy approached, the statue would turn in that direction and lower his lance, as if to charge.

Aben Habuz was impatient to try out the powers of the talisman and longed for an invasion, just as before he sighed for peace. His desire was soon granted. Early one morning the face of the bronze horseman turned in the direction of the Elvira Mountains and his lance pointed towards the Pass of Lope.

—To arms, and let all Granada be on the alert! —commanded Aben Habuz.

—My king —said the astrologer— do not alarm your city or call out your warriors to free you from your enemies. Order them to withdraw, and let's go up to the tower on our own.

They did this, and when they entered, they found the window that looked towards the Pass of Lope wide open.

—In that direction lies the danger —said the astrologer— come near and you will see the mystery of the table.

The king approached the chessboard and to his surprise he saw that all the little wooden figures were moving. The horses jumped and lifted their forelegs, the soldiers raised their weapons and there was a faint sound of drums and trumpets, the clash of steel and neighing of charging horses, all very faint, like the humming of bees or mosquitoes.

—Behold, my king! —exclaimed the astrologer—. Your enemies are advancing over those mountains through the Pass of Lope. If you want to frighten them without loss of life, strike these figures with the butt of the magic lance; but if what you want is blood and death, strike them with the point.

Pale with excitement, Aben Habuz clasped the lance and edging towards the table he exclaimed:

—I think we'll have a little blood!

Then, with the point of the lance he spiked several of the tiny figures and pushed at others with the butt; some fell dead on the board and the rest began fighting each other.

With great difficulty the astrologer was able to restrain such a pacific monarch and prevent him from finishing off all his enemies. He finally managed to persuade him to leave the tower and send out scouts to the Pass of Lope.

They returned with the news that the Christian army had advanced through the mountains almost within sight of Granada, when they began to fight one another and retreated, leaving many dead.

Aben Habuz was delighted with the success of the talisman, and exclaimed:

—At last I shall be able to live in peace, with all my enemies defeated! How can I reward you?

—My needs are few and simple: just grant me enough to furnish my cave and I shall be happy with that.

—This really wise man is not at all ambitious!

Then, with the point of the lance he spiked several of the tiny figures and pushed at others with the butt...

—exclaimed the king, pleased at such a cheap reward; he instructed his treasurer to hand over to the astrologer whatever he wanted to complete and furnish his cave.

Ibrahim ordered several rooms to be opened up in the rock, to connect up with his hall of astrology; he had them furnished with luxurious sofas and couches, with rich silks from Damascus on the walls.

—I'm an old man —he said— and I can no longer rest my bones on a stone bed, and these damp walls need to be covered.

He also had baths constructed, full of perfumes and aromatic oils.

—Baths are good against the stiffness of old age and restore freshness and flexibility to a body which is withered by study —he explained.

He asked for innumerable lamps of silver and glass, to perfume the atmosphere and shine like the daylight.

—The sunlight is too harsh for the eyes of an old man —and the light of the lamp is more adequate for the studies of a philosopher.

The treasurer complained to Aben Habuz about the huge sums of money that he demanded daily, but the king had given his word.

—Let us be patient, he said. —There is an end to everything, and to furnishing these rooms too.

His hermitage was finally completed, like a wonderful underground palace. Three days later, the astrologer once more appeared in front of the treasurer.

—I just want a little entertainment —he said—. I would like to have a few dancing girls.

— Dancing girls? replied the treasurer in surprise.

—Yes, dancing girls —answered the wise man—; and they must be young and beautiful, to delight my eyes. Just a few, since I have simple tastes and it takes very little to please me.

While the philosopher studied in his retreat, the pacific Aben Habuz spent his time in his tower, planning fierce battles. The old man found it easy entertainment making war in this way, and enjoyed himself killing off armies as though they were swarms of flies.

For some time he did whatever he wished and even made fun of his neighbours and insulted them in order to make them attack him, but in the end, in the face of so many disasters, none of them dared to invade his lands. Many months went by and the bronze horseman stayed quiet. The king began to notice this lack of amusement and he grew bad-tempered with the monotonous boredom.

One day the horseman turned suddenly and pointed his lance towards the mountains of Guadix. Aben Habuz hurried up the tower, but the magic table turned in that direction remained quiet and the soldiers motionless. He was surprised, and sent out scouts to explore the area; they returned three days later without having seen any soldiers, but with a beautiful young Christian lady who they had taken captive while she was asleep beside a fountain.

She was beautifully dressed, with pearls entwined in her long black hair and jewels which shone as brightly as her eyes; around her neck she wore a chain of gold with a silver lyre.

A shock ran through Aben Habuz as he contemplated her beauty, and he asked who she was and what her name was.

—I am the daughter of a Christian prince who was the ruler of this land. His armies were destroyed as if by magic, he has been exiled and I am now a prisoner.

—Beware, my king! —whispered Ibrahim. —This may be one of those sorcerers who deceives in the most seductive of ways. She has an air of witchcraft about her. Undoubtedly this is the enemy that the talisman pointed out.

—You may be a wise magician —answered the king, —but you are no expert in the ways of women. I know more about that question than Solomon himself, and there is nothing evil in this young lady.

—I have given you many victories by means of my talisman, replied the astrologer, but I have never shared in the booty. Give me this prisoner, and if she is really a sorceress, then I will conjure up a spell against her curses.

—What, more girls? —cried Aben Habuz—. Don't you have enough dancing girls to entertain you?

—Dancing girls, yes, but I have no singer. A little music will refresh my mind when I am tired of studying.

—Calm your desires —answered the king angrily—. This young lady is set aside for me.

The requests and protests of the astrologer were useless; he and the king were highly displeased when they parted company. The wise man retired to his retreat, even after advising the king to be careful with his dangerous captive, but Aben Habuz resigned himself completely to the enjoyment of his passion. His greatest illusion was to make himself agreeable to this beautiful Christian; although he was not young, he was rich, and an old lover is usually generous. He ransacked the Zacatín of Granada for the richest presents for the princess: silks, jewels, precious gems and exquisite perfumes. He offered her music, dancing, tournaments, bull-fights. But in spite of all this magnificence, the lover never seemed to impress the young lady. As soon as he began to declare his love for her she played her silver lyre, which undoubtedly had magical charms, because the king was immediately overcome by a deep sleep in which his passion disappeared, at least for a time. All Granada laughed at his passion and groaned at the treasures wasted on the fancies of their king.

Finally a rebellion broke out in the very capital, and the magic talisman was ineffective. The palace was surrounded by an armed mob, threatening the lives of the king and his Christian favourite. The king's warlike spirit awoke once again, he marched out with his guards, put the rebels to flight and put an end to the rebellion. Then he went in search of the astrologer, who remained shut up in his cave, full of resentment, and in the friendliest way he asked him what he should do to avoid such dangers.

—Keep that young lady at a distance, she is the cause of everything.

—I would rather lose my kingdom! exclaimed Aben Habuz.

—You will run the risk of losing both, replied the astrologer.

—Don't be hard on me and tell me some solution. I do not care for grandeur or power, all I wish for now is rest. I would like a quiet retreat to escape from the world and dedicate the rest of my life to tranquillity and love.

—What would you give me if I provide this for you? –asked Ibrahim.

—Name your reward, and if it is in my hands, you shall have it.

So the astrologer spoke to the king about the garden of Iran, one of the wonders of the happy Arabia which he had visited in his youth. It was a magnificent palace, with a garden adorned with fountains and pools, trees and flowers, and orchards full of delicious fruits. It had the peculiarity of being invisible to everyone, except when some traveller appeared and was fascinated by the view of its towers, buildings and wonderful vegetation. Afterwards it disappeared and only a desert could be seen in its place. The palace and gardens had been built by a king who wanted to be the owner of a paradise like Heaven, and because of his pride he was swept off the earth, and his work hidden from the eyes of man by a powerful curse.

—I can make such a palace and garden for you on the mountain overlooking the city, thanks to the magic of the Book of Knowledge of Solomon —said Ibrahim.

—Oh wise man! —exclaimed Aben Habuz—, make me a paradise like that and ask me for whatever you want, even though it may be half of my kingdom.

—You know I am an old philosopher who is content with little, said the astrologer; —the only thing I ask of you is the first beast of burden with its load that crosses the portal of the palace.

The king agreed to such a moderate condition and Ibrahim began his work. On the top of the hill, exactly above his underground residence, he ordered a great gateway to be built in the centre of a strong tower.

It had an outer porch with a high arch and, within it, the hall. On the keystone of the portal the astrologer engraved a huge key, and on the keystone of the outer arch an enormous hand. These were the two talismans, in front of which he spoke some words in an unknown language.

Then he shut himself away for two days in his hall of astrology, busy with his secret enchantments; on the third day he climbed up the hill, and came down late at night and presented himself before Aben Habuz.

—At last I have accomplished my work, the most magnificent palace that man can imagine. It has sumptuous halls and galleries, charming gardens, refreshing fountains and perfumed baths; the whole mountain has been converted into a paradise. Like the garden of Iran, it is protected by an enchantment that hides it from the eyes of the living beings, except from those who possess the secret of its talismans.

—At dawn tomorrow we shall go and take possession, exclaimed Aben Habuz enthusiastically.

Hardly had the rays of the sun began to shine on the Sierra Nevada when the king mounted his horse and, with a few attendants, rode up the steep hill. Beside him rode the Christian princess, with her silver lyre hanging around her neck. The astrologer walked on the other side of the king, leaning on his stick.

Aben Habuz was anxious to see the palace and the gardens, but could see nothing as yet.

—That is the safeguard of this place, said the astrologer. —Nothing of it can be discovered until you have passed the enchanted gateway and entered inside it.

At the entrance the wise man stopped and pointed out the magic hand and the key to the king.

—These are the talismans that guard the entrance

of this paradise. Until the hand reaches down and clasps the key, there will be no power capable of defeating the master of this mountain.

While Aben Habuz was contemplating everything with admiration, the princess's horse advanced towards the middle of the entrance.

—Here is my reward, cried the astrologer: the first animal with its load that crosses the magical gateway.

Aben Habuz smiled at what he thought was the old man's joke, but when he realised that he was serious, his beard trembled with anger.

—What trick is this? he said furiously. —You know very well the meaning of my promise: the first beast of burden with its load to cross through the gateway. Choose the strongest mule from my stables, load it with the most valuable of my treasures and it will be yours, but do not dare to think of the person who is the delight of my heart.

—Why should I want riches? replied the astrologer scornfully. —Don't I possess the Book of Knowledge and therefore the command of all the hidden treasures on earth? The princess belongs to me; you gave me your word and I claim her as my own.

The princess, with a scornful smile, watched from her mount those two old men arguing about the pos-

...saw the astrologer lying on a couch, listening to the sound of the magical silver lute of the princess.

session of her beauty and youth. The king's anger got the better of his prudence.

—Miserable son of the desert! cried the king. Accept me as your master and do not pretend to play around with your king.

—My master! My king! repeated the astrologer. – The king of a mole-hill wants to command over the master of the talismans of Solomon! Farewell, Aben Habuz, govern over your own little kingdom and enjoy your paradise of fools, and I will laugh at you in my retreat.

Saying this, he took the horse's bride, struck the earth with his stick, and he and the young princess sank through the centre of the gateway. The earth closed behind them without leaving a trace.

Aben Habuz ordered a thousand workmen to dig in the place where the astrologer had disappeared, but it was useless: the stony hill resisted their tools, also, when they dug a little, the earth fell in again as it was dug out. He looked for the entrance of the cave that led to the astrologer's underground palace, but he could not find it. What had once been a door was now hard rock.

With the disappearance of Ibrahim, the benefit of his talismans came to an end. The bronze horseman remained still in the direction of the hill and pointing with his lance to the place where the wise man had sunk, as if the worst mortal enemy of Aben Habuz were there.

Sometimes some faint music could be heard in that place, and the voice of a woman too. One day a country man informed the king that the night before he had found a crack in the rock, entered into an underground hall and saw the astrologer lying on a couch, listening to the sound of the magical silver lute of the princess.

Aben Habuz searched for the crack, but it had now closed. He tried once more to unearth his enemy, but in vain, because the curse of the hand and the key was too powerful to be broken by men. As regards the summit of the mountain, site of the promised palace and garden, it remained as bare as a desert; either the so-called paradise was hidden to human eyes or it was just the astrologer's lie. People imagined it was the latter, and called the place *The king's madness* or *The paradise of the madman*.

To make the misfortunes of Aben Habuz even worse, the rival neighbours, who he had provoked, humiliated and destroyed at his will, invaded his territory, since they knew that it was no longer protected by the magic spell, and the most pacific of monarchs spent the rest of his life in the midst of constant struggles.

Aben Habuz finally died and was buried, centuries ago. The Alhambra was later built on this famous hill, and to a certain extent, the fabulous delights of the garden of Iran were also carried out. The enchanted gateway still exists, protected by the hand and the key. This is now the Gate of Justice, main entrance to the fortress. Beneath this gateway, so it is said, the old astrologer still remains in his underground hall, lulled by the princess's silver lyre.

The sentinels who stand guard there often hear music on summer nights and sleep peacefully. Even those who stand guard by day doze on the stone benches of the entrance or under the nearby trees. According to the legends, this will continue for centuries to come. The princess will remain captive of the astrologer and the old man will remain prisoner in his magical dream, until the day of Judgement or until the hand grasps the key and the spell is broken.

Prince Ahmed al Kamel or the Pilgrim of Love

The Generalife

Prince
Ahmed al Kamel
or the Pilgrim of Love

*T*here was a Moorish king of Granada who had only one son, named Ahmed, called by his courtiers *al Kamel* or the Perfect. Astrologers predicted that he would be an excellent prince and a fortunate king, but that he would have an amorous temperament, which would result in serious risks; however, if he was able to avoid these until he became of age, these dangers would disappear and he would lead a happy life.

For this reason, the king decided to educate the prince where he would never see a woman nor hear the word love. To this purpose he built a magnificent palace on the hill above the Alhambra, surrounded by beautiful gardens but enclosed by walls —which we now call the Generalife—. The young prince was shut in there, under the vigilance of Eben Bonabben, a wise and severe old man from Arabia, who had lived and studied in Egypt and who was more attracted by a mummy than by the most tempting of beautiful women.

—Take all precautions, said the king, —but if my son gets to learn anything about love while he is with you, you will answer with your head.

The serious old man, Bonabben, smiled at this warning.

—Rest assured, your majesty. What lessons can I give about that useless passion?

Under the care of the philosopher, the prince grew up in the palace and its gardens. In his service he had slaves who were mutes, who neither knew love nor would they have been able to talk about it. Eben Bonabben tried to teach him the mysterious science of Egypt, but the young prince had little interest in it, although he hid his boredom, listened to the long lessons and even acquired a smattering of knowledge. So he reached the age of twenty, with the knowledge which corresponds to a prince, but completely ignorant of love.

About this time, he began to behave differently. He abandoned his studies and began walking through the gardens and meditating beside the fountains. He had learnt a little music and also he liked poetry. The wise man was alarmed at this and tried to distract him away from these hobbies with a course in algebra, but he rejected it angrily.

—I can't stand algebra, he —said—. I need something that reaches my heart.

Here is the end to all reasoning, —thought Bonabben—. The prince has discovered that he has a heart!

He watched closely over his pupil and saw that his natural tenderness was active and only needed some way to showitself. Ahmed felt disturbed, without knowing why. Sometimes he indulged in wonderful fantasies or played touching music on his lute; at other times he stroked his favourite flowers or carved his name in the bark of a tree.

Eben Bonabben was alarmed at seeing that his pupil was about to discover the forbidden science, and he shut him in the highest tower of the Generalife, high above the delights of the garden, which were so dangerous for the sensitive Ahmed.

To entertain him in his solitude, he began to teach the prince the language of birds, which he had learnt in Egypt, and the prince was so fascinated with this that he soon knew as much as his master.

Now he had companions with whom he could converse. The first one was a hawk, that dived on his prey from the battlements. But he was common pirate of the air, a show-off who did nothing but boast of fierce deeds.

His new friend was an owl that spent the day in a hole in the wall and only went out at night. He thought himself to be very wise, and talked about astrology and dark sciences, so then the prince found him even more boring than Eben Bonabben.

Next, he got to know a bat that hung from its legs in a dark corner until twilight. He knew very little, laughed at what he didn't know and nothing satisfied him.

There was also a very talkative swallow, that was restless and always flying about; seldom did he stop for long enough to maintain a conversation. Ahmed understood that he was rather shallow and pretended to know everything without really knowing anything at all.

The tower was too high for other birds to visit it. The prince soon grew tired of these friendships and returned to his loneliness. The winter went by and spring arrived, and with it the happy time when birds look for a mate and make their nests. From the woods and gardens of the Generalife there could be heard a whole chorus of birdsong, repeating continuously the same theme of love in every variety of note and tone. Ahmed, high up in his tower, listened in surprise. "What can this *love* be, of which I know nothing?

He asked the hawk, who replied scornfully:

—Ask the vulgar birds, that are born to be prey to us, the masters of the air. I am a warrior, and I know nothing of what they call love.

So the prince asked the same question to the owl, that looked back at him with offended dignity.

—I spend my nights studying and my days meditating in my retreat —he replied—. I never listen to the insignificant singing birds, and I have no idea what this thing called *love* is.

He turned to the bat again, and asked him the same question.

—When I fly, all the birds are asleep —he grunted— and I have never worried about their affairs. I am neither bird nor beast, and I have no idea of this thing called *love*.

Finally he went in search of the swallow, that was in a great hurry, as always.

—I have thousands of visits to make, and a thousand affairs to settle, so I cannot waste my time with nonsense. I am a citizen of the world, and I have no idea what this thing called *love* is.

The young prince was disconcerted by these doubts, when his aged guardian entered the tower.

—Oh tell me, Eben Bonabben! —exclaimed Aben Ahmed, full of curiosity—, what is this thing called love?

Bonabben was struck as though by lightning.

—Where have you learnt such an idle word, my prince?

Ahmed led him to the window. The nightingale was singing to his loved one among the roses; a continuous hymn to love arose from the grove.

—God is great! —exclaimed the wise man—. How is it possible to hide from man this secret that even the birds can reveal?

Then he turned to the young man and said:

—Close your ears to those dangerous songs. Love is the cause of hate and bitterness. Let Allah preserve you!

The old man withdrew hurriedly, leaving poor Ahmed very confused. "There is such happiness in their singing – he said, listening to the birds trilling away. If love is the cause of unhappiness and disagreement, then why are those little birds not sad and tearing each other in pieces, instead of fluttering and playing among the flowers?

One morning he was lying on his bed, when a dove, pursued by a hawk, flew in through the open window and fell on the floor. The pursuer, making fun of him, flew off towards the mountains.

The prince picked up the poor little bird and stroked it, offering it white wheat and pure fresh water, but the dove rejected them with pitiful moans.

–What's the matter? –the young man asked him–. Don't you have everything you could wish for?

–Oh no! Aren't I separated from my partner in this season of love?

–Of love! –exclaimed Ahmed–. Can you tell me, what is love?

–It is the torment of one, the happiness of two and the discord of three; it is a charm which gives happiness to two when they are together, and makes them unhappy when they are separated. Are you not joined to anyone by these bonds of affection?

–I like my master Eben Bonabben, but sometimes I find him boring and I feel better without him.

–I don't mean that, I mean the great mystery and the beginnings of life. The whole of nature is full of it, the most insignificant bird, beetle and butterfly are happy in love. Is there no other creature of another sex who has captured your heart?

—Where can I, in my loneliness, find that person you speak about? sighed Ahmed.

Their conversation continued, and so ended the first lesson of the prince, who freed the bird, telling him.

—Fly away and rejoice with your partner. Why should you remain enclosed in this prison, where love will never enter?

The dove flew swiftly off. The singing of the birds made the young prince feel even sadder, now that he knew its meaning.

When he saw Eben Bonabben again, he shouted at him in anger:

—Why have you not revealed to me what even the smallest of insects knows? Why have you let me waste my youth without the joys of love?

The wise man realised that Ahmed now knew about the forbidden science, and he told him the astrologer's prophecies and the care that had been taken to avoid the risks threatening him.

—Now —he added—, my life is in your hands. If the king discovers what you have learnt, I shall pay with my head.

The young man was really fond of Eben Bonabben and he agreed to hide this knowledge, so as not to put him in danger.

A few days later, while he was wandering through the leafy avenue, the dove he had freed flew down and alighted on his shoulder.

—Where have you been since we separated? — he asked the prince.

— In a distant country, from where I bring you news as a reward for the freedom you gave me. During my long flight, one day I observed a garden surrounded by walls, on the banks of a stream; beside it was a meadow, where there was a splendid palace. I perched on a branch, where I saw a princess of unsurpassable beauty enclosed between those high walls, and I thought: "Here is the creature destined by Heaven for my prince".

His heart throbbed with passion on hearing this description, and Ahmed wrote a message of love to the young princess, bewailing his imprisonment that prevented him from going in search of her. He also added some poems and addressed the letter to The Unknown Beauty, from the Captive Prince Ahmed; then he perfumed it and handed it over to his friend.

—Away you go and do not rest until you have delivered this letter to the maiden of my heart!

...saw a pearl necklace around its neck, and hanging from it was a small picture with the portrait...

The dove darted away like an arrow and the prince watched until it disappeared behind the mountains.

Ahmed waited in vain, day after day, for the return of his messenger. He began to accuse him of ingratitude, when one afternoon the dove flew into his room and fell dead at his feet. A hunter's arrow had pierced his heart, but even so, he had struggled to the end to accomplish his mission. On bending over him, the sad prince saw a pearl necklace around its neck, and hanging from it was a small picture with the portrait of a beautiful young lady. Undoubtedly this was the unknown princess of the garden, but who was she, and where was she? Had she sent this portrait as proof that she accepted his love? The death of the dove left everything in mystery.

The young prince gazed sadly at the portrait. "What a beautiful face. You look at me as though you would encourage me, but where can I find you? Who knows the distance that separates us and the misfortunes which may threaten us!"

Then Ahmed took his decision: "I shall flee from here and search for the unknown princess throughout the world, as a pilgrimage of love".

The palace was not strictly guarded during the night, because nobody suspected any kind of attempt from the prince; that was all right, but how was he to find his way around in his escape by night, without knowing the country? He remembered the owl, who flew by night and who should be in the know regarding the paths and secret passes, so he went to consult him.

—You must know —replied the owl proudly— that we are an ancient and numerous family, which has come down in the world, but we are still owners of ruined castles and palaces throughout the whole of Spain. When visiting my relations, I have got to know all these hiding places.

The prince was overjoyed and begged him to accompany him on his amorous escapade.

—Not a hope! exclaimed the angry owl. —Am I a bird to occupy my time with questions of love, I who have dedicated my life to meditation and worship of the moon?

—Consider that while you are contemplating the stars, your talent is lost to the world. One day I shall be king and I'll be able to give you a place of honour.

Although the owl considered himself to be above these everyday necessities of life, he was ambitious, so he agreed to escape with the prince and serve as his instructor.

Ahmed collected all his jewels in order to pay for the expenses of the journey, and that same night he lowered himself from the tower by a rope, climbed the Generalife walls and, under the guidance of the owl, made his escape, reaching the mountains before dawn.

—I would recommend going to Seville, said his colleague. Many years ago, on a visit to the city by night, I came across a tower where there lived an old crow from Egypt. I advise you to look him up, because he is a fortune-teller and a sorcerer, and he is very knowledgeable.

The prince accepted his advice and started out towards Seville. He travelled by night and rested during the day in a dark cave or ruined tower, because his guide had a passion for ruins, like an archaeologist.

When they reached the city, the owl, that hated the light and the noise of the streets, remained on the outskirts, in a hollow tree.

Ahmed entered the city and discovered the tower, which stood out above the houses. It was the same tower as still exists, known as the Giralda.

The prince went up the tower and found the old, mysterious, grey-haired crow that had lost most of his feathers and had a film over one eye, which made him look rather phantom-like. He stood on one leg, looking with his good eye at a geometrical design drawn on the floor.

—Excuse me, wise and venerable crow —said the young prince, with fear and respect —excuse me if I am interrupting your studies that astonish the whole world. I am in search of the lady in this portrait, and I beg you to tell me where I can find her.

—I only visit the old and decrepit —said the crow dryly, — and not the young and beautiful. I croak news of death and I fan my wings beside the sick people. Go elsewhere to search for news of your beautiful unknown princess.

—Where can I search, other than among the sons of wisdom? I am a prince chosen by the stars for a venture on which the future of empires may depend.

When the crow realised the enormous importance of the affair, his changed his tone and listened carefully to the story. Then he said:

—I can give you no information about that princess, as I do not usually fly over the gardens frequented by ladies, but if you go to Cordoba, under Abderahman's palm tree, in the courtyard of the mosque, you will find a great traveller who knows many queens and princesses. He will tell you the news you are looking for.

Ahmed said farewell and left Seville, met up with the owl in the hollow tree and together they set out for Cordoba.

When they reached the gates, the bird flew into a hole in the wall and the young prince entered, in search of the palm tree planted in olden times by Abderahman in the centre of the great courtyard of the mosque. Monks and Muslim holy men sat together in groups and the faithful followers purified themselves in the fountains.

At the foot of the palm tree there was a ring of people listening to someone who was talking excitedly. "This must be the person who can inform me about the unknown princess", said the prince to himself.

He mixed with the crowd and marvelled at a talkative parrot, with brightly-coloured plumage, typical crest and a haughty look, and seemingly very satisfied with himself.

—This parrot, one of those present pointed out to him —has all the oriental wisdom at the tip of his tongue, he tells stories, recites verses, and is famous in foreign courts, where all the women admire him.

The prince asked to speak to this illustrious traveller in private, and he was granted an interview, but the bird burst out laughing when he heard the reason for his pilgrimage; he explained that just the mention of the word love made him laugh.

— That is old-fashioned, he said, we no longer hear distinguished people talking about love.

Ahmed realised that the parrot wanted to boast of being noble, since he had lived in the court, and he asked him straight away if he knew the princess in the portrait.

—What a pretty face, he exclaimed examining the miniature. This is undoubtedly Princess Aldegunda, one of my favourite friends.

—Where can I find her?

—She is the only daughter of the Christian King of Toledo, replied the parrot, and she remains hidden from the world until her seventeenth birthday, because of the prophecies of certain astrologers. Nobody can see her, neither can you.

—I am the heir to a kingdom, Ahmed told him confidentially—. Help me to achieve the princess, and I will trust you with an important post when I am king.

I shall be delighted! But it must be something that doesn't need much effort, because we wise men are horrified at work.

They left Cordoba, and the young man, the owl and the parrot set out together on their journey.

Their progress was slow, because the aristocratic bird disliked getting up early, while the night bird liked to sleep at midday and wanted to visit all the ruins they came across. The parrot laughed at the seriousness of the owl, who felt offended and refused to speak to him for the rest of the day. The joker and the philosopher were always quarrelling.

In this way they crossed the mountains of Sierra Morena, the plains of La Mancha and Castile, they followed the banks of the River Tagus and finally came in sight of a walled city on a mountain, with the river flowing at its feet.

—There is the city of Toledo, famous for its antiquities, said the owl. —Look at those legendary towers, where my ancestors spent their time in meditation.

—What do we have to do with legends and antiquities? interrupted the parrot. Look, my prince! There is the mansion of youth and beauty, the abode of the princess you are searching for.

Ahmed saw a stately palace between the trees of a garden, in the green meadows on the banks of the River Tagus. This was the place described to him by the dove, and he saw that it was surrounded by high walls patrolled by armed guards.

The prince turned to the parrot: —You have the gift of speech, fly to the princess and tell her that Ahmed, the pilgrim of love, has arrived to claim her.

The parrot flew away to the garden and alighted on the balcony of a pavilion, where he saw the princess on a sofa, crying and with her eyes fixed on a piece of paper.

—Dry your tears, he said. —I am here to bring happiness to your heart.

The young princess was startled to see a bird dressed in green and bowing to her.

—What happiness can you bring me, if you are no more than a parrot?

—I have comforted many beautiful ladies in my life, answered the parrot, angry at her question. —But never mind that... Ahmed, Prince of Granada, has arrived in search of you.

On hearing these words, the eyes of the young princess lit up.

—That is indeed happy news, because I felt ill with doubt about the loyalty of Ahmed. Tell him I have his letter and his poetry engraved in my heart, and that he must prove his love for me by force of arms. Tomorrow is my seventeenth birthday; my father is holding a tournament and the prize for the winner will be my hand in marriage.

The parrot flew off on his return journey. The prince felt full of happiness on having found his faithful and beautiful princess, but at the same time he was worried about the approaching tournament. The suits of armour were shining and the trumpets of those who had arrived in Toledo to participate were resounding.

The same star had controlled the destiny of both the prince and the princess; she was hidden away from the world until the age of seventeen to protect her from love, but the fame of her beauty reached far beyond her isolation. Several princes wished for her hand in marriage and the king trusted this to the luck of the combat. There were princes of great strength and skill among the rivals, while Ahmed lacked in arms and was also unskilled in their use.

—How unfortunate I am! Oh Eben Bonabben, why didn't you instruct me in the management of arms? he complained.

Faced by these lamentations, the owl took up the conversation, and said:

—In a cave in the nearby mountains there is a suit of armour and a horse, both magical, which I discovered a long time ago. They belonged to an Arab magician, and on his death, he left them there under a spell, and they can only be used by a Muslim between sunrise and midday. The person who uses them during that time will conquer any enemy.

—That's enough, let's search for that cave! Exclaimed the prince.

Guided by his advisor, he entered the cave, hidden in a rocky peak, and there was the magic suit of armour with a lance; beside it stood an Arab steed, as still as a statue. The armour shone like in olden days, and the horse pawed the ground and neighed with joy when Ahmed stroked his neck. Now, well prepared with a horse to ride and a weapon, the prince decided to take part in the tournament.

The eventful day arrived. The venue for the combat was prepared below the walls of Toledo, where the platforms and stands had been set up. All the beauties of the land were assembled there, while the knights who were to fight rode around in the country. The incredible beauty of Aldegunda eclipsed the rest when she appeared for the first time in front of the gaze of the crowd, and the princes who were contending for her hand awaited the combat even more ardently.

However, the princess was pale and nervous while watching the crowd of knights. The trumpets were about to sound the start when the herald announced a stranger. Ahmed arrived with a steel helmet covered with pearls, golden armour, his scimitar and dagger adorned with precious stones. He carried a round shield and brandished the magic lance. The rich adornments of his mount hung down to the ground, and the animal neighed with delight before the shiny weapons. The arrogant appearance of the young prince, announced as the Pilgrim of Love, sent a shiver through the beautiful ladies.

As only princes were admitted to the tournament, Ahmed declared his name and noble birth, but a Muslim could not take part in a contest where the hand of a Christian princess was the prize.

His rivals observed him with a menacing look. One proud, strong man laughed at his romantic nickname and the angry prince challenged him to fight. At the first contact with the magic lance, the strong knight fell from his horse. Ahmed's mount charged against the group and the lance knocked down everything it encountered, completely out of the prince's control. The young prince was carried off into the fields, knocking down everyone, left and right, nobles and common people, while to himself he regretted his involuntary heroic deeds. The angry king sent out all his guards, who were immediately disarmed. So he himself took hold of the shield and lance and charged, to intimidate the foreigner with his royal majesty, but Ahmed's horse and the magic lance respected nobody, neither the king nor the dignitaries. To his own amazement, Ahmed felt himself thrown against the king, who flew into the air, while his crown rolled in the dust

At this moment the sun reached its midday peak, the magic lost its power and the horse galloped across the plain, swam across the Tagus, and arrived at the cave, where it once more became as motionless as a statue. Ahmed dismounted, took off his armour and sat in the cave, meditating on the desperate state in which he found himself. How could he show his face in Toledo after causing such humiliation to the knights and the king? What would the princess think of such an outrage? Full of anxiety, he sent his messengers in search of news.

The parrot returned with a horde of gossip. The princess had been taken to the palace in an unconscious state and everybody was talking about the incredible feats of the Muslim knight. Some said he was a Moorish magician or a demon in human form, while others related traditions of enchanted warriors in the mountain caves, and all of them agreed that no mere mortal could have carried out such a feat.

The owl flew by night to inspect the royal palace. He returned at daybreak to recount to the prince what he had seen.

—I was watching from one of the towers of the palace, when I saw from a window the princess, lying on her bed surrounded by servants and doctors, denying help or advice from any of them. When they all left, she took a letter out from her bodice, read it and kissed it, and began to cry so bitterly that even I, in spite of being a philosopher, could not help feeling moved.

—How true your words were, Eben Bonabben! exclaimed Ahmed, distressed. What worries and sorrows afflict the loved ones. Let Allah protect the princess from this thing they call love!

Later reports confirmed the owl's tale. Toledo was gripped with confusion, the princess was taken to the highest tower of the palace, and all the avenues were closely guarded. The young princess was the victim of terrible grief, which nobody could explain, nor could the doctors cure it. She was thought to be under a magic spell, and the king promised the most precious jewel from the treasury as a reward to whoever could cure her.

—It will be a happy man who manages to cure her, if he knows how to choose from everything in the royal treasury, said the owl when he heard this proclamation.

—What do you mean? asked Ahmed.

—During one of my nightly rounds of Toledo I came across an association of archaeological owls, which met up in the tower where the king's treasure was kept. They were particularly interested in the chest that contained the silk carpet of King Solomon's throne.

— I have heard Eben Bonabben talking about the wonders of that talisman, said the prince. If I could gain possession of that carpet, I would be sure of my happiness.

The following day he disguised himself as a poor Arab from the desert, so that nobody should recognise him as the warrior who caused such a scene in the tournament. With a shepherd's flute in his hand, he went towards the royal palace, where he announced himself as candidate for the reward for curing the princess. The guards tried to throw him out as a vagrant, but on hearing the protests, the king ordered him to be brought before him.

—Before you, said Ahmed, you have a Beduin from

the desert, which is inhabited by demons and malign spirits which torment the shepherds at night. Our best remedy against them is music.: we have ancient songs which drive them away. If your daughter is possessed by one of them, I promise you that I will free her from the spirits.

The king became hopeful again when he heard these words, and he took the young prince to the room of the princess. The half-opened windows opened on to a terrace, and there was the sad young lady, rejecting all types of advice.

The prince sat on the terrace and played on his flute several Arab tunes which he had learnt in the Generalife. The young princess remained motionless, while the doctors smiled scornfully. Then Ahmed began to sing the verses of the letter in which he had declared his love.

The princess recognised the song, she listened and her heart was filled with joy. The king ordered Ahmed to be led into her presence. The lovers discreetly exchanged looks, which spoke more than volumes. Never had the triumph of music been so complete: colour returned to the cheeks of the princess, the freshness to her lips and the sparkle to her eyes.

–You will from now on be the first doctor of my

...the carpet rose into the air taking away the prince and the princess.

court, and I will take no other medicine than your music. As a reward, receive the most precious jewel from my treasury.

—My king! replied the prince, you have a coffer in your treasury containing a carpet; give me that, and I shall be happy.

Everyone was surprised at the modesty of the Arab. They brought the coffer and took out the carpet, which was of a fine green silk, covered in Hebrew and Chaldaic characters. The physicians laughed at the simplicity of this new folk healer, who was content with such a small payment.

—This carpet, said Ahmed, covered Solomon's throne, and it is worthy of being placed before such beauty.

So he spread it out on the terrace, under the sofa that had been brought for the princess, and sat at her feet and said:

—Who can defy fate? The astrologers' prophecy has been fulfilled. Your daughter and I have loved each other in secret for a long time. I am the Pilgrim of Love!

At these words the carpet rose in the air, taking away the prince and the princess. The king and the doctors watched open-mouthed, until it became a tiny speck in the horizon and finally disappeared into the heavens.

The king shouted angrily at his treasurer: — How could you allow an infidel to possess such a talisman?

—Your majesty, we did not know its qualities. If it is indeed Solomon's carpet, then it has magical powers and can transport whoever possesses it through the air.

The king assembled a powerful army and set off in pursuit of the fugitives. After a long march, he camped in the Vega and the King of Granada himself came out to meet him; he recognised him as the Arab singer, since Ahmed had inherited the throne on the death of his father, and Aldegunda was his sultana.

The Christian king soon calmed down when he saw that his daughter was allowed to continue as a faithful follower to her beliefs, and that there were festivities and rejoicing instead of battles. So the king returned to Toledo, and the young couple reigned happily and wisely in the Alhambra.

The owl and the parrot made their return journey to Granada separately. As a recompense for their services, Ahmed named the owl his prime minister and the parrot his master of ceremonies. Never has there existed a kingdom more wisely administered, nor a court better organised in the rules of etiquette.

Avellano Fountain

Hill of the Sun

The Moor's Seat
(old Moorish fort)

Valley of the Darro River

GENERALIFE

ALBAYZÍN

Chinos Hill

ALHAMBRA

Central Alhambra walk

Gomérez Hill

New
Square

Zacatín

Bibarrambla
Square

CITY

E

N

S

W

The Moor's Legacy

The Square of the Cisterns

The Moor's Legacy

There is an esplanade in the Alhambra called the Square of the Cisterns (la Plaza de los Aljibes), so called because of the underground water reservoirs, which have existed from the time of the Moors. In one corner of the esplanade there is an Arab well cut into the rock, and it is very popular in Granada for its cool, clear water. The water carriers, with water-jars on their shoulders or earthenware vessels on their donkeys, came up and down the steep slopes from morning to night.

Around this same well there was a perpetual club formed by invalids, old women and unoccupied people from the fortress. There they gossip, ask the water-carriers for news from the city and comment on everything that is seen or heard; housewives and lazy maid-servants with their water-jars on their head or in their hand whisper about the latest gossip.

Among the water-carriers who used to come to this well there was a short, strong man, with wide shoulders and twisted legs, called Pedro Gil, or Perejil for short, from Galicia.

Perejil the Galician had begun to work with a water-jar on his back; gradually he prospered, until he was able to buy a strong and long-haired donkey that he loaded up with his vessels protected with fig leaves against the heat of the sun. There was not such a merry water-carrier in the whole of Granada. While he walked behind his donkey he shouted out the typical cry heard in Spanish cities in the summer: *¿Quién quiere agua? Agua más fría que la nieve! Who wants water? Water colder than snow!* When he served a customer a glass of water it was always with a pleasant word, and if it was a lady, with a compliment or a mischievous smile. This honourable Galician was considered the kindest and happiest of mortals, but his kind aspect hid a mound of worries and problems. He had several ragged and hungry children who were always screaming for food, and a wife who wasted his scarce earnings on nonsense or on taking away his donkey to go and enjoy herself on Sundays and holidays, which are almost as numerous as working days in Spain. On top of all this, she was a bit slovenly and lazy, and above all, a chatterbox who used to abandon her obligations to go and gossip with the neighbours.

Perejil put up with the wastefulness of his family patiently and as meekly as his donkey carried the water-jars, and although he sometimes protested in private, he never dared to question the virtues of his slovenly wife.

He loved his children, who were like him, small and strong, wide-shouldered and bandy-legged. Perejil's greatest pleasure, when he had a day of rest and a few coins to spend, was to take them all out among the orchards of the Vega, while his wife stayed behind, dancing with her friends next to the River Darro.

It was late one summer night and most of the water carriers had finished their work. It had been an extremely hot day, and the moonlight tempted people to stay out in the fresh air to enjoy the cool of the night. There were still customers to drink water, so Perejil, thinking of his hungry children, thought: "I will take one more trip to the well, to earn the Sunday lunch". So, once more, he went up the Alhambra hill.

When he reached the well he found a solitary stranger dressed in Moorish clothes, sitting on a bench

...she stepped forward like an angry hen defending her chicks.

in the moonlight. Perejil paused and looked at him in surprise, and a little frightened, but the stranger signalled to him to approach.

—I am ill, he said; take me to the city and I will give you double what you can earn with your water-jars.

The water carrier felt touched with compassion. God forbid that I should ask for any payment for an act of humanity.

So he helped him on to his donkey and set off for Granada. When they arrived he asked him where to take him.

—I have no house or room, exclaimed the Moor in a faint voice. Allow me to spend the night in your house and you will be well rewarded.

Therefore Perejil found himself with an infidel as a guest, but he could not deny him hospitality in such a sad state, so he took him to his dwelling. When they saw the stranger with a turban, the children fled and hid behind their mother. She stepped forward like an angry hen defending her chicks.

—Who have you brought home, to draw the attention of the Inquisition? she shouted.

—Be quiet, wife, replied the Galician. He is an ill, homeless man, without any friends; would you be capable of leaving him to die in the street?

His wife would have continued protesting, but for the first time Perejil was firm, and he settled the Muslim on a mat in the coolest part of the house, as this was the only bed that he could offer in his poverty.

In a brief pause between the convulsions that attacked him, the Moor spoke to the water carrier in a low voice.

—My end is near. If I die, I leave you this box as a reward for your charity, he said, showing him a little sandalwood box that he hid under his cloak.

He wanted to add something more, but his convulsions began again, even more strongly, and after a short while, he died.

His wife became mad with anger.

—What will happen to us when they find the body in our house? We shall be sent to prison as murderers, she said.

Perejil also felt afraid and he almost regretted having done a good deed, but finally he had an idea:

—It still is not daylight. I will bury him outside the city, on the banks of the River Genil. Nobody saw him come in here, and nobody will know anything of his death.

With the help of his wife, he wrapped up the body

in the mat, put it across the donkey and went in the direction of the river.

As bad luck would have it, opposite the water carrier there lived a barber called Pedrillo Pedrugo, a gossip and a wicked man, always alert to what was happening around him. He was a sort of scandalous chronicler for the busybodies of Granada, and he had more customers than all the other barbers. The meddling barber heard Perejil arrive late at night, and the exclamations of his wife and children. Peering out of the window, he saw him take the man dressed as a Moor into his house. Before daybreak, he saw the water carrier leave with his laden donkey. He was so intrigued that he dressed rapidly, followed the Galician at a certain distance, and saw him dig a hole in the sandy banks of the Genil and bury something that looked like a body.

As soon as the sun came up, the barber rushed to the house of the mayor, who was a daily customer of his, to shave his beard.

—What strange things happen! he exclaimed! Robbery, murder and burial all in one night!

—What are you saying? shouted the mayor.

—I am saying that Perejil the Galician has robbed, murdered and buried a Moor tonight, replied the barber, as he applied the soap.

—But how do you know that?

—Be patient, sir, and you will hear everything about it. Pedrillo did two things at the same time: shave the mayor and tell him about the robbery, murder and burial of the Muslim.

This mayor was the greediest man in Granada, and he set such a high value on justice that he sold it at its weight in gold. He imagined that this robbery must be important, and wondered how to put it all in the hands of the law. Just trapping the guilty man would be feeding the gallows, but trapping the booty would make the judge rich and this, in his opinion, was the main purpose of justice. So he called the bailiff, a thin man with a black top hat with the brim turned up, black clothes and cloak, which made him look even skinnier, and a dreaded cane in his hand. This legal bloodhound acted so rapidly that he caught poor Perejil before he returned home, and he took him and his donkey before the authorities.

—Listen, you miserable fellow! Roared the mayor with a voice that made the poor Galician's knees shake. You deserve to be hung as a punishment for your crime, but I am merciful and ready to listen to reason. The man who was murdered was an infidel, an enemy to our religion. No doubt you killed him in a fit of religious enthusiasm, so I will be lenient with you; hand over what you robbed and we shall forget the whole matter.

The water-carrier called on all the saints to witness his innocence, and told the story of the dying Moor, but it was useless.

—Do you insist that he had neither gold nor jewels, which were the object of your greed? asked the judge.

—He had nothing more than a little sandal-wood box, which he gave me as a reward for my services, replied the poor man.

—A sandal-wood box! —exclaimed the mayor, imagining precious jewels—. Where have you hidden it?

—It is in one of the panniers of my donkey, and is at the services of your lordship.

The bailiff brought the mysterious box. The mayor opened it and they all gathered around to see the treasures it contained, but inside it there was nothing but a parchment scroll written in Arabic and a bit of candle.

When the mayor saw that there was no booty, he listened impartially to the water-carrier's explanations and the declarations of his wife, and as he was convinced of his innocence, he released him and let him keep the box, though he kept the donkey in payment of the costs.

Once more the unfortunate Galician had to carry the water himself, climbing up the Alhambra hill to the well with the water-jar on his shoulder. In the heat of the summer midday he lost his usual good humour.

—That dog of a mayor! he shouted, robbing a poor man of his means of living and of his best friend! My poor donkey, I am sure you have not forgotten your old master, and you must be missing those water-jars!

At home, his wife and her complaints were always waiting for him, because she had warned him not to carry out that noble act of hospitality, and now she took advantage to humiliate him. If their children needed food or clothes, she would tell them scornfully:

—Go to your father, he is the heir to the King Chico (the Little King) of the Alhambra; ask him to give you the treasure hidden in the Moor's box!

The unlucky Perejil used to suffer, both in body and soul, but he patiently put up with this cruel taunting. But one night, after an exhausting day's work, when he was insulted once again, the poor man lost his temper and he threw the sandal-wood box on the floor.

—What an unlucky day it was when I set eyes on this box and sheltered its master under my roof! he cried.

As the box struck the floor, the lid opened and the parchment rolled out.

Perejil looked at it in silence. Who knows, maybe this writing is important, if the Moor guarded it with such care?

The next morning he went into the shop of jewels and perfumes in the Zacatín belonging to a Muslim from Tanger, and asked him to explain the Arabic words to him.

—After a lot of reading, I see that this manuscript, he said, is the enchantment for recovering a hidden treasure, which is at present under the spell of a sorcerer. – It has such strength that neither locks, bolts nor rocks will yield before it.

—What does that matter to me? said the water-carrier. I don't know a word about hidden treasures. But that night he came across a group of people around the well in the Alhambra; there they talked about wonderful old legends and enchanted treasures. Everybody believed that there were wonderful treasures hidden under the floor of the Tower of the Seven Floors.

These stories made a deep impression on our friend, the honest Perejil. "And what if there is a hidden treasure under the tower and this parchment were to help me to get hold of it!"

That night he tossed and turned, and hardly slept

a wink. Bright and early he went to the Moor's shop
and told him what was passing through his mind.

—You can read Arabic, he said. Suppose we went
to the tower together and tried out the spell. If it fails,
we have nothing to lose, and if it succeeds, we can
share everything we discover.

—Wait! Little by little! replied the Muslim. This
writing has to be read at midnight by the light of a
special candle. Without that candle, the manuscript
is useless.

—I have it, and I will bring it immediately! cried the
Galician. He ran home and returned with the piece of
yellow wax which he had found in the sandal-wood box.

—This is just the kind of candle specified in the
manuscript, said the Moor. – While it burns, it will open
walls and caves, but woe betide he who remains inside when it burns out; he will be enchanted together
with the treasure.

Late that night, when nobody was awake except the
owls and the bats, they went up the Alhambra hill to
the mysterious tower. Lighting their way with a lantern, they reached the entrance to a vault. Trembling
with fright, they descended some steps cut in the rock
leading to a dark and empty chamber. More stairs took
them to deeper vaults. In this way they descended sev-

eral flights which took them to even deeper chambers, one after the other. The floor of the fourth was solid; according to tradition, there were three more underneath, but a strong enchantment would not let them continue downwards. The air here was damp and cold, had an earthy smell and the light hardly shone. They stopped, breathless and uncertain till they heard the clock strike midnight faintly from a tower. Then they lit the wax taper, which gave out a perfume of myrrh, incense and strange perfumes.

The Moor began to read the manuscript. Hardly had he finished when he heard a sort of underground thunder, the floor opened and disclosed another flight of steps. Trembling with fear, they descended to another vault covered with Arabic inscriptions. In the centre was a huge chest, with an enchanted Moor standing motionless on either side. In front of the chest were jars filled with gold, silver and precious jewels. They put their arms up to the elbow into the biggest one, taking out handfuls of coins, bracelets, ornaments and necklaces of oriental pearls. While they filled up their pockets they glanced nervously at the enchanted Moors, who watched them without blinking an eyelid, grim and motionless. Frightened by some imaginary noise, they finally ran upstairs, falling over each other on the higher floor and

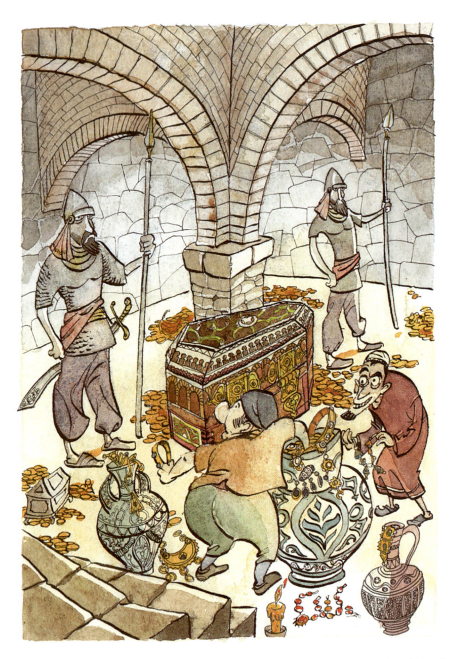

They put their arms up to the elbows into the biggest one, taking out handfuls of coins...

extinguishing the candle. The floor closed again with a terrible sound like a thunder clap.

They were terrified, and they did not stop until they had left the tower and could see the stars shining through the trees. Then they divided up the spoils, happy enough with what they had taken, but determined to return and drain the jars to the bottom. To make sure of their good faith, one of them kept the manuscript and another the candle; then they set off for Granada, happy at heart and with their pockets well filled. The wary Muslim advised them to keep everything top secret until all the treasure was secured, to avoid the news reaching the mayor, and the water-carrier agreed.

—My friend Perejil, said the Moor, you are a discreet man and you know how to keep quiet, but you have a wife.

—She will not hear a word about this.

—All right, I shall depend on your discretion and your promise.

This was a sincere enough promise, but what man is capable of hiding a secret from his wife? When poor Perejil returned home, he found his wife crying.

—At last you are back after spending all night on the streets! she cried as he walked in. I am surprised you have not returned with another Moor as a guest! What is to become of me? I have a husband who no longer brings home bread for his family and who is out day and night with the unbelieving Moors! We shall have to go out begging!

Perejil felt sorry for her, so he put his hand in his pocket and brought out a few coins for his wife. Before she could recover from her surprise, he took out a chain of gold and dangled it in front of her, laughing with delight.

—What have you done, Perejil? exclaimed his wife. You must have killed someone and robbed them! Scarcely had this occurred to her when she imagined the prison and the gallows and her little bandy-legged Galician hanging there, and she became hysterical.

To calm her down, the water-carrier had no alternative than to tell his wife the story of his good fortune, which he did after she made him a solemn promise to keep it a tight secret.

There are no words to describe his wife's delight. She flung her arms around her husband's neck and almost strangled him with her enthusiasm.

—Now what do you say about the Moor's legacy? asked Perejil. In the future, do not insult me when I try to help someone in misfortune.

The Galician retired to bed and slept profoundly. However, his wife emptied his pockets on the mat and sat down to count the coins and tried on the necklaces and earrings.

The next morning, Perejil took one of those big coins to a jeweller in the Zacatín, and pretended he had found it among the ruins of the Alhambra. The jeweller realised that it was the purest gold and offered him a third of its value, but the water-carrier was quite happy with that. He bought new clothes, toys and provisions for a splendid meal, and returned home, where the children danced around him, while he considered himself the happiest of fathers.

His wife faithfully guarded the secret for a whole day and a half, in spite of feeling her heart about to burst in the face of her gossiping neighbours. True enough, she could not avoid presuming about the expensive clothes she had ordered, and commenting on her husband's intention of leaving his job as water-carrier, since it was bad for his health. She also mentioned that she would spend the summer in the country, as she could not live in the town during such a hot season.

Her friends thought she had taken leave of her senses, and as soon as she turned her back, they laughed at her airs and graces and elegant gestures.

Although she may have been restrained outside, inside her house she made up for it, trying on strings of pearls, Moorish bracelets and diamond diadems, admiring herself in her rags in a broken mirror. In a moment of vanity, she could not resist showing herself in front of the window to enjoy the effects of her finery on the passers-by.

As luck would have it, the curious barber, Pedrillo Pedrugo, was at that moment sitting in his shop and he saw the sparkle of the diamonds. He recognised the water-carrier's wife, and went quickly off in search of the mayor, then Perejil was once again taken in front of the judge.

—You told me that the infidel who died in your house had left nothing more than an empty box, the mayor shouted furiously, and now I discover that your wife is dressing herself up in pearls and diamonds. Get ready to return everything and to swing from the gallows!

The poor water-carrier fell on his knees and told the tale of how marvellously he had acquired his fortune. The mayor, the bailiff and the barber all listened eagerly to his tale. The bailiff sent for the Moor who had helped with the enchantment; nearly scared out of his wits, when he saw the water-carrier, who looked at him with an ashamed face, he understood everything.

—You miserable beast! he said, —didn't I warn you not to tell your wife anything?

The stories of both colleagues coincided exactly, but the mayor pretended not to believe them and threatened them with prison.

—Mr. Mayor, said the Moor astutely and quietly, —nobody else except us knows anything about the affair, and there is still enough in the cave to make us all rich. Promise a fair share and all will be opened; if it is refused, the cave will remain closed forever.

The bailiff took the mayor aside and recommended him to promise what he asked for until he could get hold of all the treasure, and later to silence the protests of Perejil and his accomplice, threatening them with burning at the stake as heretics and infidels.

The mayor approved of the advice, and turning towards the Moor, he said:

—Tonight you will repeat the charm in my presence. If such a treasure exists, we shall share it out in a friendly way, and nothing more will be said of the matter. In the meanwhile, you will remain under arrest.

The Moor and Perejil agreed willingly, convinced that the result would prove that their words were true.

About midnight the mayor, the bailiff and the barber set out, accompanied by the Moor, the water-carrier and the donkey to carry the treasure. They reached the tower, tied up the donkey to a fig tree and went down to the fourth vault.

They took out the manuscript and the Moor read it in the candlelight. The earth trembled like the first time and the floor opened with a noise like a thunder clap, showing the steps. The mayor, the bailiff and the barber were terrified, and did not have enough courage to descend. The other two went down, found the two Moors just as they were before, silent and motionless, and they took two jars full of gold coins and precious stones, which the water-carrier took up one by one on his shoulders; in spite of being used to carrying heavy weights, it was a great effort for him. He was sure that his donkey could not manage more weight.

—This is enough for now, said the Moor; here we have sufficient to make us all rich.

—What, is there still more treasure down below? asked the mayor.

—The richest of all, answered the Moor: an enormous chest full of pearls.

—Let's bring up that chest some way or other, cried the greedy mayor.

But the two colleagues flatly refused; one insisted that they already had sufficient, the other wouldn't load his donkey with any more, in case he should break its back.

So the mayor turned back towards his followers and gave them some orders.

—Help me to bring up the coffer and let's divide up the share between us.

At this he went down the steps, helped by the bailiff and the barber.

When the Moor saw that they had gone right down, he blew out the candle, the floor closed with the usual crash and the three avaricious men were shut away. Then he and the water-carrier hurried out into the open air together.

—What have you done? cried Perejil; the mayor and the others have been shut into the vault.

—That was Allah's will! cried the devoted Moor.

—And aren't you going to let them out?

—Allah forbids it! The writing goes that they are to remain enchanted until some future adventurer breaks the charm.

Saying this, he threw the candle-wax into the bushes.

They returned to the city with the well-loaded donkey, and the modest water-carrier did not know what gave him the greatest pleasure, winning the treasures or having regained his donkey.

The two colleagues divided up the treasure into equal parts. The Moor, who appreciated the jewels more, kept the largest part of the pearls and precious stones, while the water-carrier was left with the wonderful solid gold jewels worth five times more.

To avoid all danger, they left for far away lands to enjoy their riches. The Moor returned to Tangiers, his native city, and the Galician travelled to Portugal with his wife, his children and his donkey. He became an important person, wore doublet and hose, a plumed hat and a sword by his side; he dropped his family name *Perejil* and changed it for the more grandiose name of *Don Pedro Gil*. His children grew up strong and happy, although they were short and bandy-legged, while his wife, *Señora Gil*, became a rather strikingly and conspicuous figure with her fringes, brocades and laces from head to toe, and rings on all her fingers.

The mayor and his cronies remained shut up under the floor of the Tower of the Seven Floors, and there they still remain, bewitched. Whenever there is a need for mean barbers, rascally bailiffs and corrupt mayors, they may be found there, but in the meanwhile their enchantment will last till the Final Judgement.

The
Three Beautiful
Princesses

The Castle of Salobreña

The Three
Beautiful Princesses

A long time ago there reigned in Granada a Moorish king called Mohammed, who was nicknamed *el Hayzari*, or *The Left-handed*. Some believe he was called this because he was really better with his left hand than with his right; other people thought it was because he used to do everything back to front, or put his foot in everything. For one reason or another he was always in trouble: he lost his throne three times, and on one occasion he had to escape to Africa disguised as a fisherman to save his life. However, he was as courageous as he was crazy and, although he was left-handed, he wielded his scimitar so well that he always managed to recover his throne by means of fighting. But instead of learning from his misfortunes, he became even more stub-

born. The disasters that were caused by him are re-
counted in the Arab chronicles of Granada; this legend is only about his private life.

One day Mohammed was riding with his followers
at the foot of the Elvira mountains, when he came
across a band of horsemen who were returning from a
raid in Christian lands. They carried a large amount
of booty and many captives of both sexes, among
whom there was a beautiful young lady, who particularly attracted his attention; she was richly dressed and
cried continuously, without paying any attention to the
comforting words of her ladies' companion.

The king was captivated by her beauty, and he knew
from the captain of the troops that she was the daughter of the governor of a fortress that they had sacked,
so he took her to the Alhambra to console and comfort her. The king wanted her to become his queen,
but the young maiden rejected him, because he was
an infidel, an enemy of her country, and worse still,
he was too aged!

The king realised that it was useless to continue in-
sisting with her, so he decided to attract the favour of
the young lady's companion who had been captured
together with her. She was of Andalusian origin, her
Christian name is not known, but the Moorish legends

call her the discreet Kadiga, and it seems that she really was discreet, as history proves. They held a secret conversation, after which she decided to defend the king's cause with her young mistress.

—Why so much sadness? she said: Isn't it better to be mistress of this beautiful palace than to live shut away inside your father's old tower. And what does it matter if Mohammed is an infidel? You are marrying him, not his religion; if he is rather old, the sooner you will become a widow and free to do whatever you wish. It is better to be a queen than a slave and to sell your wares at a good price than have them taken from you by force.

Her arguments were successful: the young lady became the wife of Mohammed the Left-handed and accepted his religion. Her discreet companion immediately became a fervent Muslim, and continued in the service of her mistress, using the Arab name of Kadiga.

In time, the king became the father of three daughters, born at the same time, and he summoned his astrologers to read his horoscope.

—Oh dear, your daughters will need special vigilance when they reach a marriageable age. You must keep them closely under your wing, and do not trust them to anybody.

This news worried Mohammed the Left-handed considerably, and he trusted to the astrologers to protect his daughters and avoid Fate.

The queen had no more children and she died a few years after the triple birth, trusting her young daughters to the loving and faithful Kadiga.

Many years went by before the princesses reached a marriageable age, but the king decided to take precautions and ordered them to be brought up in the Castle of Salobreña, a palace situated high on a hill overlooking the Mediterranean. Here, the Muslim monarchs shut away their relatives who might put their safety in danger. This was where the princesses lived, shut away from the world, but living in comfort. There were gardens full of fruit and flowers, aromatic bushes and perfumed baths. On three sides the castle overlooked a green valley, bordered by the Alpujarra Mountains, and the other side looked out to sea.

In this wonderful place, with a pleasant climate and under a cloudless sky, the princesses grew up and, although they were educated in the same way, they soon developed a different character. The eldest was called Zaida, the second one Zoraida and the youngest Zorahaida, as there had been exactly three minutes difference between their births.

Zaida was courageous, always taking the lead in everything, just as she was the first to be born, curious and rather nosy.

Zoraida was passionate about beauty, she enjoyed gazing at herself in a mirror or in a fountain and she loved jewels and tasteful adornments.

Zorahaida was sweet and shy and highly sensitive. She spent hours on a balcony, watching the stars or the moonlit sea, and a fisherman's song or the distant sounds of a Moorish flute were enough to give her the greatest pleasure. But any disturbance of nature terrified her and a clap of thunder made her faint.

The years went quietly by, and the discreet Kadiga looked after the three princesses.

One of the walls of the Castle of Salobreña reached down to a rock overhanging the sea, with a narrow, sandy beach at its foot. On this rock there was a pavilion with latticed windows through which the sea breeze blew in, and where the princesses used to spend the hot midday hours.

One day the curious Zaida was there, while her sisters were having an afternoon sleep, when her attention was drawn by a galley which was rowing along the coast. It was full of armed men, and anchored at

...a group of soldiers landed with several Christian prisoners.

the foot of the tower, where a group of soldiers landed with several Christian prisoners. Zaida woke her sisters and they peeped through the latticed windows. Among the prisoners were three Spanish gentlemen, young, elegantly dressed, noble looking and walking proudly, in spite of their chains and their enemies. The princesses, who lived shut away in a castle among servants, were fascinated, and they gazed excitedly at these three handsome men.

—Could there be a more noble person than that knight dressed in crimson? said Zaida. He walks as though he were surrounded by slaves!

—Look at that one dressed in green! —exclaimed Zoraida—. What grace and what elegance!

Zorahaida said nothing, but secretly she preferred the knight dressed in blue.

When the prisoners were out of sight, the three princesses sighed sadly, looking at one another and sitting on their couches, lost in thought.

They were sitting like this when Kadiga found them; they told her what they had seen, and even her hardened heart was moved by what they told her.

—Poor young men! she exclaimed. Their captivity has no doubt left some broken-hearted ladies in their country! My children, you cannot imagine the life that those gentlemen lead in their country! The tournaments, serenades and courting!

Zaida's curiosity was aroused, and she listened excitedly to the *dueña's* animated descriptions of her native land. While she listened to the comments on the charm of the Spanish ladies, Zoraida discreetly looked at herself in the mirror. Zorahaida could hardly help sighing on hearing about the moonlight serenades.

The old lady repeated her tales every day, until she realised the harm that she was doing. She had not considered the fact that the princesses had grown up and were now at a marriageable age. "It is time to advise the king," she thought.

One morning Mohammed the Left-handed was in the Alhambra when a slave from Salobreña arrived, with a message from Kadiga, congratulating him on his daughters' birthday. He brought a little basket decorated with flowers, with a peach, an apricot and a nectarine, all fresh, beautifully-coloured and temptingly ripe. The king was well aware of the language of fruit and flowers, and immediately guessed the significance of the present. "The time mentioned by the astrologers has arrived: my daughters are at a marriageable age. They are hidden and guarded by the discreet

Kadiga, but not under my custody. I must collect them under my wing and not trust them to anybody."

So he ordered a tower to be prepared in the Alhambra and he set out for Salobreña to bring them back personally. Three years had gone by since the last time he saw his daughters, and he found them wonderfully changed. During that time the princesses had gone through the stage of girlhood to being young women. Zaida was tall and well-formed, with firm steps and a penetrating look, and she bowed to Mohammed as a king rather than as a father. Zoraida, of medium height, an attractive look and extraordinarily beautiful, smiled at her father, then she kissed his hand and recited a poem. Zorahaida was shy and quiet, shorter than her sisters and with a tender beauty that seemed to be in search of fondness and protection. She hesitated as she approached her father and would have kissed his hand, but when she saw his smiling face she forgot her restraint and threw her arms round his neck.

Mohammed the Left-handed contemplated his three beautiful daughters with pride and surprise.

—Three daughters, and all of them at a marriageable age. This tempting fruit needs a dragon as a guard!

For the return journey to Granada, he ordered everybody to keep off the streets where they were to pass through and all the doors and windows to be kept shut as the princesses drove past. Then they set off, escorted by a troop of horsemen.

The three princesses, their faces covered with veils, rode on snow-white horses with rich trimmings and silver bells that tinkled at every step. But woe betide the person who might stop on the way to listen to the tinkling! The guards had orders to kill them.

Near Granada, the cavalcade came across some soldiers who were escorting a group of prisoners. There was not enough time to step aside from the road, so they lay with their faces to the ground and ordered the captives to do the same. Among them were the young knights who the princesses had seen from the pavilion, and either from pride or because they had not understood the orders, they remained standing and contemplating the approaching group.

The monarch was full of rage and was about to give a deadly blow with his scimitar when the princesses, even the timid Zorahaida, begged for mercy for the prisoners.

—Your majesty, said the captain of the guard, these are three noble gentlemen who have fought like lions in battle. They are of very distinguished descent and may be worth a ransom.

—I will spare their lives, said the king, but take them to Vermilion Towers, and make them do forced labour.

Mohammed was committing another of his errors. In the confusion, the three princesses lifted their veils and their beauty had the desired effect. In those days people fell in love more quickly than now, as all the old stories tell us, so the knights were completely captivated. Curiously enough, each of them was enchanted with a different princess. They in turn admired the courage and attitude of the prisoners even more.

The cavalcade continued its journey. From time to time the young princesses glanced cautiously back, in search of the Christian prisoners who were taken to their prison in the Vermilion Towers.

The residence prepared for the princesses was a tower apart from the main palace of the Alhambra, although it connected with it by the wall that surrounded the whole summit of the hill. One side gave on to the interior of the fortress and had a small garden at its foot. The other side overlooked a deep valley separating the Alhambra from the Generalife. Inside the tower there were delightful small rooms, surrounding a lofty hall decorated in bright colours. In the centre there was a fountain surrounded by flowers, and a refreshing trickle of water. Hanging around the hall there were birds in gold and silver cages.

The princesses had always been cheerful in the Castle of Salobreña, and the king expected to see them as happy in the Alhambra, but they became sad. The scent of the flowers was no delight to them, the song of the nightingale interrupted their dreams at night, and the eternal murmuring of the fountain tried their patience.

At first this made the king irritable, but he thought about it and said: "They are no longer children, they are grown women and they need suitable amusements. So he called the dealers from the Zacatín, who brought silk dresses, cashmere shawls, diamond and pearl necklaces, rings, bracelets and all types of jewels.

This was to no avail. In the midst of all this luxury, the princesses looked like three languishing flower buds drooping on their stems. The king had no idea what to do, faced by the whims of these young marriageable ladies, and for the first time in his life, he asked for advice; he applied to the experienced ladies' companion.

—Kadiga, he said, I know that you can be trusted. I want you to discover the secret illness affecting the princesses, and to find the way to make them happy again.

Kadiga promised to obey him and to try and win the confidence of the young ladies.

—My dear girls, why are you so sad in such a beautiful place?

The princesses gave a long and melancholy sigh.

— What more do you want? Would you like me to bring the wonderful parrot that speaks all languages? Or a monkey from Gibraltar to amuse you with its tricks? But Zaida and Zoraida were displeased and rejected these offers.

—And what about the famous black singer Casem? They say he has a fine voice.

—I have lost all interest in music, said the delicate Zorahaida.

—You would not say that, replied the old lady wickedly, if you had heard the music of the three gentlemen who we met on the journey. But, bless me, my dears, why are you blushing like that?

—It's nothing; carry on, continue!

—Well, as I went past the Vermilion Towers last night I saw the gentlemen, who played the guitar and sang. They did it so well that I could not help being moved at hearing the song from my homeland. Three such noble young men, chained up like slaves.

The kind old lady could not help shedding some tears.

—Perhaps you could arrange for us to see them, said Zaida.

—A little music would cheer us up a lot, added Zoraida.

Zorahaida said nothing, but she threw her arms around Kadiga.

—What are you saying? exclaimed the old lady. Your father would kill you! Undoubtedly they are very distinguished and well-educated young men, but they are enemies of our faith and you should hate them.

The princesses begged her even more, and declared that a refusal would mean their broken hearts.

What could she do? How could she allow the hearts of three princesses to be broken just for the strumming of a guitar. Also, although she had changed her religion, she felt certain nostalgia for the Christian religion, so she decided to satisfy the young ladies' wish.

The captives were under the orders of a bearded renegade called Hussein Baba, easy to be bribed. Kadiga paid him a secret visit, and slipped a large gold coin into his hand as she said:

—Hussein, the three princesses, who are so in need of amusement, have heard of the musical talents of the three Spanish gentlemen and would like to listen to them. I am sure you will not deny something so simple and innocent.

–And let them hang my head on the top of the tower! That is the reward the king would give me if he were to discover it.

–There is no danger: we shall make the princesses happy without him knowing it. Set the Christians to work in the steep bank that passes under the tower and during their breaks, let them play and sing. In this way my young ladies will hear them, and I shall pay you well.

Then the old lady dropped another golden coin in his rough hand.

Her eloquence was irresistible. The next day, the three knights set to work in the steep bank. In the mid-day heat they sat at the foot of the tower and sang accompanied by the guitar.

It was a steep bank and the tower was high, but their voices rose high and clear in the silence. The princesses had learnt the Spanish language from their ladies' companion and they were moved by the tender words of the song. The discreet Kadiga, on the contrary, felt decidedly nervous.

–Let Allah protect us! she exclaimed. They are singing a love song to you. How dare they! I shall ask them to be thoroughly beaten.

—What! Beat those poor knights for singing so tenderly?

The three beautiful sisters were horrified at the idea and, in spite of her real indignation, the good old lady easily calmed down. Besides, the music had had a beneficial effect on her young mistresses; they once more had a rosy colour in their cheeks and a sparkle in their eyes, so she no longer protested at the love song.

When the captives finished, Zoraida took up her lute and chanted a little African song that said: Although the rose is hidden among her petals, she listens with delight to the song of the nightingale.

From then onwards the knights worked there almost every day. A sort of mysterious conversation revealing their mutual feelings was set up between the prisoners and the princesses through these songs. The young ladies leaned secretly over the balcony or communicated with the knights through the symbolic flower language that they both knew. The difficulties added to the charm, because love grows stronger in the face of obstacles.

The change in his daughters surprised and delighted

the Left-handed King, but nobody was as happy as the discreet Kadiga, who put it all down to her skills.

But then there was an interruption in this communication, when the young men no longer appeared in the ravine. The three beautiful girls leaned over the balcony in vain and sang like caged nightingales, to no avail: their loved ones were not to be seen, and not a note was heard in reply. Kadiga went in search of news and returned full of confusion.

Oh, my children! she exclaimed. You can hang up your lute. The Spaniards have been ransomed, they have gone down to Granada and are preparing to return to their native country.

The princesses were in despair at what they considered the knights' disloyalty.

—This is the way of the world, said Kadiga. When you are as old as I am, you will realise what men are like. I am sure that these young men have their loves in Cordoba or Seville, and they will soon be serenading them without remembering the beautiful Moorish ladies in the Alhambra. Discard them from your hearts.

These words only increased the distress of the princesses, who remained inconsolable for two days. On the morning of the third day, the old woman entered their rooms fuming with anger.

—Never speak to me again about your Spanish knights!

The princesses asked her anxiously what had happened.

—They have proposed treason to me, the most faithful of all servants! she cried.

They have dared to propose that I convince you to run away with them to Cordoba and become their wives!

The astute old woman covered her face with her hands and gave way to an attack of anger. The three sisters' faces changed colour, they trembled and looked at each other out of the corner of their eyes. In the meanwhile, Kadiga continued:

—How is it possible that I have lived to be insulted in this way! Me, the most faithful of all servants!

In the end, the eldest princess, who always took the initiative, went up to her and said:

—Mother, if we were willing to flee with the Christians, would that be possible?

The good old woman restrained her grief sharply. —Of course it is possible! Haven't the knights already bribed Hussein Baba and prepared the whole plan with him? But how can you deceive your father, who has placed his confidence in me!

Once again the old woman succumbed to another attack of despair.

—Our father never put any trust in us, replied the eldest sister. He shut us up and treated us like prisoners.

—Yes, it has been really shameful to shut you up in this old tower, replied Kadiga, once more containing her grief, so that you wilt like roses in a vase. But, to flee from your native country...!

—The land where we shall flee to is our mother's native country, where we shall live in freedom, with young husbands instead of an old, severe father!

—That is true, too! You have a tyrannical father. But are you going to leave me here to suffer his vengeance?

—By no means, Kadiga. Can't you come with us?

—Certainly I can. When I spoke to Hussein Baba he promised to look after me if I accompanied you. But are you willing to renounce your father's faith?

—The Christian religion was our mother's first faith, said Zaida; and both she and her sisters were willing to accept it.

—I am glad to see you on the way to salvation, exclaimed the old woman happily, because I was born a Christian and I have made up my mind to return to

If we wait, we shall be lost! Come on down, princess, or we shall leave without you!

my faith. Hussein Baba, who is from a nearby village to mine, also wishes to return and be reconciled to the Church. The gentlemen have promised that they will provide generous help for us if we marry.

In short, it seems that this provident old woman had already made plans with the Christians and the renegade about the whole flight. Zaida accepted immediately and her sisters followed suit. True enough, the youngest one doubted between the daughterly feeling of duty and youthful passion, but the eldest of the two won the day, so Zorahaida also prepared for the flight.

The Alhambra hill has old underground passageways through the rock, leading towards different parts of the city and to the banks of the Darro and the Genil, where the Moorish kings escaped from sudden rebellions or went off on their own private ventures. Through one of them, Hussein Baba had decided to take the princesses out of the town, where they would meet the knights with horses, ready for the flight to the border.

The appointed night arrived. The Tower of the Princesses was locked up and the Alhambra remained silent. At midnight, Kadiga listened from the balcony of a window for the renegade's signal from the garden, tied a ladder to the balcony and lowered herself down it, followed by the two eldest sisters. But Zorahaida was indecisive. She turned her eyes to the room where she had been imprisoned like a bird in a golden cage, but safe. What dangers would be awaiting her in the wide world? She thought of her horse and immediately put her foot on the step, but then she thought of her father so she drew it back again. Doubt was pounding in the heart of the young princess who was in love, but at the same time, ignorant of life.

In vain her sisters implored her, the old ladies' companion scolded her and the renegade swore; the young princess wavered indecisively.

Every moment the risk of discovery was greater. Distant footsteps could be heard.

—The patrols! cried the renegade. If we wait, we shall be lost! Come on down, princess, or we shall leave without you!

Zorahaida was desperately upset. She loosened the ropes and let them fall in despair.

—Flight is now out of the question! she exclaimed. Let Allah guide and bless you!

The two older sisters did not want to leave her, and they would happily have stayed, but the patrol guards were drawing near and Hussein pushed them along the underground passage. Hurriedly they felt their way blindly through a labyrinth cut in the heart of the mountain and reached the outside of the walls, where the Spanish knights were waiting.

The lover of Zorahaida was desperate, but there was no time to waste. The two princesses mounted side-saddle behind their lovers, the discreet Kadiga mounted behind the renegade and they set off at top speed towards the Pass of Lope which leads through the mountains towards Cordoba. They immediately heard the sound of drums and trumpets in the Alhambra. They spurred their horses on and galloped across the flat plain of the Vega at the foothills of Sierra Elvira; the renegade paused and listened.

—For the moment there is nobody in our pursuit and we can escape to the mountains.

At that moment an intense light shone on top of the Alhambra watch-tower.

—Look! cried Hussein. The sign of alarm for the guards of the passes! Come on! There is no time to be lost!

While they galloped along the road going round the Elvira Mountains, the fire on the Alhambra tower was answered by other fires from all the towers.

Forward! On to the bridge before the alarm reaches there! shouted the renegade swearing loudly.

When they arrived in sight of the Puente de Pinos, which crosses a strongly flowing river, the watchtower lit up with lights and the glitter of coats of armour. Hussein Baba signalled to the knights, left the road and plunged into the river, followed by the others. They were swept down river a little by the raging current, but the princesses held on to the horsemen firmly and they all reached the other bank safe and sound. Guided by the renegade they crossed the mountain through the roughest passes, avoiding the regular roads. They finally reached the ancient city of Cordoba, where their return was celebrated with great rejoicing, since the knights came from the noblest families. The princesses became converted to Christianity and were happy wives.

In the hurry to help them in their flight, we have forgotten to mention the discreet Kadiga. Galloping across the plain she had clung like a cat to Hussein, but when she rode into the river on horseback, she was frightened beyond recognition.

—Don't clutch me so tightly! shouted Hussein Baba, hold on to my belt, and do not be afraid!

But when the renegade stopped on the top of the hill to catch his breath, the old woman had disappeared.

—What has happened to Kadiga? the princesses asked in alarm.

—Only Allah knows! answered Hussein. My belt came loose and Kadiga was swept away down the river. Let Allah's will be done! Although it was a belt of great value.

—The princesses cried disconsolately the loss of their advisor, but that excellent old lady had only left half of her seven lives in the water. A fisherman pulled her on to land, astonished at his miraculous catch. Legends do not tell what happened to her afterwards, although it is known that she showed her discretion in not letting herself fall into the hands of the Mohammed the Left-handed.

Nor do we know much about the reaction of the monarch when he discovered everything. It was the only time he had asked for advice, and he never did it again. As for Zorahaida, she is believed not to have regretted staying in the Alhambra. Sometimes, from the walls of the tower, she gazed sadly towards Cordoba; other times, she gently sang songs lamenting her loneliness. She died young, and according to popular rumour, was buried in a vault under the tower.

The following tale, to a certain extent, seems to have arisen from the one we have just told.

The Rose
of the Alhambra

The Tower of the Princesses

The Rose of the Alhambra

After the surrender of Granada by the Moors, the Spanish kings often resided there, until they fled under the menace of the continuous earthquakes, which destroyed houses and shook ancient Moorish towers.

For many years the palaces of the Alhambra remained silent and closed, while the gardens were neglected. In the Tower of the Infantas, where the three princesses once lived, cobwebs covered the vaults and bats and owls nested in the rooms that in other times had been graced by the presence of Zaida, Zoraida and Zorahaida. The neglect of the building may be due to the superstitions of the neighbours; there was a rumour that the spirit of Zorahaida, who died in that tower, was seen by moonlight, sitting beside the fountain in the hall or crying high in the battlements, and that at midnight the gentle notes from her silver lute could be heard.

Royalty finally returned to the city of Granada: Philip V, the first Bourbon on the throne of Spain and his wife Isabella, Princess of Parma. The Alhambra was repaired and fittingly decorated to receive the illustrious guests. The arrival of the court changed the aspect of the palace that had been deserted for so long. The noise and activity outside recalled the previous splendour of the fortress. Inside the palace, the rustling of dresses could be heard, the murmuring voices of the courtiers, the coming and going of servants and ladies-in-waiting in the gardens and the sound of music.

Among the members of the royal followers was a favourite page of the queen, called Ruíz de Alarcón. He was just eighteen years old, light, graceful and handsome. In front of the queen he was very respectful, but at heart he was a mischievous youth, spoiled by the ladies of the court and more experienced with women than was to be expected for his age.

One morning the page was wandering through the groves of the Generalife with one of the queen's hawks, which he had taken to amuse himself. While he was walking along, he saw a bird that flew out of the undergrowth, so he let his bird of prey loose. The hawk fell on its quarry, but it escaped from its claws, and the hawk flew off without paying any attention to the page's calls. It alighted on a remote and solitary tower of the outer walls of the Alhambra, on the edge of the valley that separates it from the Generalife; it was the Tower of the Princesses.

The page descended into the valley, but could find no entrance to the tower, so he went round it to the side facing inside the walls.

In front of the tower there was a small garden and he opened the little gate, crossed by some clumps of roses and reached a door which was locked and bolted. Through a crack in the door he saw inside; there was a little hall with Moorish decoration, marble columns and an alabaster fountain surrounded with flowers. In the centre hung a cage with a little singing-bird; on a chair lay a cat among reels of silk and other sewing things, and a guitar was propped up against the fountain.

Ruíz de Alarcón was surprised at this show of feminine taste of elegance in a tower that he imagined was deserted. Then it reminded him of the legends of enchanted halls in the Alhambra, and wondered if the cat might be the spellbound princess.

He knocked on the door and a beautiful face

peeped out of a little window high up, but disappeared immediately. He waited in vain, but heard no
footsteps inside, only silence. Had he imagined it,
or was this apparition the fairy of the tower? He
knocked again, more loudly, and once again the
beautiful face appeared; it was a beautiful fifteen-
year-old damsel.

The page whisked off his feathered hat and asked
her with the greatest politeness to allow him to go up
and retrieve his hawk.

—I dare not open the door to you, *señor*, said the
young lady, blushing: my aunt has forbidden it.

—I beg you, young lady. I cannot return without
the queen's favourite hawk.

—Are you from the court then?

—Yes, and I shall lose everything if I lose that hawk.

—It is precisely to you gentlemen from the court
who my aunt has forbidden me to open the door.

—But that is intended against the wicked gentlemen. I am just a harmless page, who will be ruined if
you deny me this small favour.

The young damsel was touched, and she thought it
would be a pity that this young fellow should be ruined for such an insignificant thing. No doubt this
young man was not one of those dangerous creatures

whom her aunt had described to her. He seemed very charming, begging her so politely, cap in hand!

The cunning page realised that she was in doubt, so he repeated his arguments, until finally the young lady opened the door with a trembling hand; he had been charmed by her face at the window, and now that he saw her from top to toe, he was felt completely and utterly enchanted.

Her clothing set off her youthful figure even more. She wore her shiny hair with a parting in the centre and decorated with a freshly-cut rose, as was customary in the country. Her skin, a little tanned, enhanced the colour of her cheeks and heightened the sparkle in her melting eyes.

Ruíz de Alarcón observed everything in one quick glance, but he did not want to lose a moment so, with a slight mention of thanks, he leapt up the spiral staircase.

He soon returned with the hawk. In the meantime, the young girl had sat down by the fountain, winding silk, but in her confusion she had dropped a reel. The page stopped down to pick it up and, still on one knee, offered it to her and when she stretched out her hand to receive it, he kissed it fervently.

—*Ave María, señor*! exclaimed the damsel blushing, since she had never before received such a greeting.

The young man apologised, assuring her that it was the correct way to express respect, and her anger, if that was what she felt, quickly disappeared. However, she continued to feel ashamed, and she sat blushing as she looked down at her sewing, tangling up the reel that she was trying to wind.

The young page was aware of her confusion and would have liked to take advantage of her, but his arguments dried on his lips, his attempts at gallantry were clumsy and ineffective; the page who had always been graceful and confident among the experienced ladies of the court, was surprised to feel insecure and speechless in the presence of a young damsel of fifteen.

The naive young maiden had better guardians in her modesty and innocence than in the bolts and bars ordered by her vigilant aunt. But what woman has a heart that is insensitive to the first whispers of love? The young maiden, in all her ingenuity, understood instinctively what the page had been unable to express, and her heart throbbed on seeing a lover at her feet for the first time. And what a lover!

Ruíz de Alarcón was beginning to recover his confidence when he heard a shrill voice at a distance.

—It's my aunt, she is returning from mass! cried the frightened young maiden. Please leave.

—No, not until you give me the rose from your hair, as a souvenir.

—Take it, but please go now.

The page took the flower, at the same time covering her hand with kisses. He placed the rose in his cap and with the hawk on his wrist he left, carrying with him the heart of young Jacinta.

When Jacinta's aunt arrived, she noticed her niece's agitation and some confusion in the hall, but a few words of explanation satisfied her.

—A hawk flew in here, in pursuit of its prey.

—Good heavens! A hawk in the tower! Have you ever seen such cheek? Even the bird is not safe in its cage!

Fredegunda was an aged spinster, who felt both terror and distrust in what she called the "*opposite sex*". It was not that she had suffered any disappointment, as nature had given her the protection of her face that did not allow any approach to her; but women who have little to fear for themselves are always ready to keep guard over their more attractive neighbours.

Her niece was the orphan of an officer who died in the wars, so she had been educated in a convent and only a short while ago had been entrusted to her aunt, under whose close care she was vegetating like a rose

...took the flower, covering her hand with kisses...

among thorns. This is not an accidental comparison, because her beauty had conquered everybody, in spite of living shut away, and following the poetical Andalusian custom, she had been given the name of Rose of the Alhambra.

The wary aunt watched over her young niece cautiously while the court remained in Granada, and she was very pleased with the success of her vigilance. It is true that the strumming of a guitar or the love songs that floated up from the moonlit groves sometimes made her nervous. Then she would encourage her niece to turn deaf ears, persuading her that was one of the tricks of the *opposite sex* to deceive young maids. But what good was such advice against a moonlight serenade?

King Philip cut short his stay in Granada and suddenly departed with his entourage. When Fredegunda lost sight of the last banner of the royal procession she returned happily to the tower, but to her great surprise she found a horse in front of the garden gate and was horrified to see an elegant young man kneeling at her niece's feet. At the sound of her footsteps he said a tender farewell to the young maiden, leapt over the wall, sprang on to his horse and rode out of sight.

Jacinta threw herself into her aunt's arms, full of grief, and crying her heart out.

—Oh, poor me! she cried, he's gone, I shall never see him again!

—Who has gone? Who is that young man who I saw at your feet?

—One of the queen's pages, who came to say farewell to me.

—A queen's page, child! repeated Fredegunda in a nervous voice. When did you get to know him?

—The hawk that entered the tower one morning was the queen's, and he came in search of it.

—Well, there are no hawks as dangerous as those pages, who make little birds like you their prey.

At first the old aunt was angry as she realised how this tender relationship had developed between the two lovers almost under her eyes, in spite of her watchfulness. But she was relieved to know that her niece had come out unharmed and victorious in the face of the "*opposite sex*" without bolts or bars, so she was convinced that the triumph was due to her prudent and cautious advice.

So the spinster aunt prided herself in her advice, and her niece remembered how she had promised to be faithful to her lover. But what is the love of a restless and nervous man? It is like a stream that caresses briefly the flowers on its banks and flows on, leaving them behind in tears.

Autumn went by, winter arrived, spring and summer returned and nothing was heard of the page.

Poor Jacinta became sadder and sadder; she abandoned her previous occupations and amusements, her reels of silk, her guitar, her flowers; she no longer listened to the birdsong and her eyes were swollen with crying.

There is nowhere as romantic as the Alhambra to foster the passion of a forlorn young damsel. It is a real paradise for lovers, but how hard to feel alone and abandoned there!

My child! said the chaste and sensible Fredegunda to her disconsolate niece. What could an orphan like you expect of someone from a noble family? Even though he was sincere, his father would forbid him marriage with someone from such humble roots. Put such vain hopes out of your mind.

Late one summer night, when her aunt had already retired to rest, Jacinta sat alone beside the alabaster fountain, just where the faithless page had knelt and kissed her hand for the first time. Her heart felt overwhelmed by these memories, and tears began to roll

down her cheeks and fall drop by drop into the fountain. The water began to get turbulent, bubbles formed
and the figure of a woman, richly dressed in Moorish
clothes rose up in front of her.

Jacinta was terrified and fled out of the hall. The
following morning she told her aunt what she had seen,
but Fredegunda took it as a dream.

—You must have been thinking of the story of the
three Moorish princesses, she said, and therefore you
dreamt of them.

—I know nothing about that story.

—You must have heard about Zaida, Zoraida and
Zorahaida who were shut up in this tower and who
decided to run away with three Christian knights.
The first two managed it, but the third sister was
lacking in courage and, according to the stories, she
died here.

—Ah, now I remember hearing that tale, said
Jacinta, and I even remember feeling sorry for the unlucky Zorahaida.

—Zorahaida's lover was one of your ancestors, explained her aunt. He wept for his lover for a long time,
but time cured his wounds and he married a lady from
whom you are descended.

Jacinta was thoughtful. "What I have seen is no fantasy, I am sure. And if it is in fact the spirit of Zorahaida that is lingering in this place, what do I have to fear?

About midnight, when everything was silent, she returned to the hall. As the distant clock tower of the Alhambra struck twelve, the fountain began bubbling up and the Moorish lady appeared again. She was young and beautiful, adorned with jewels and with a silver lute in one hand. Jacinta was about to faint, but on hearing her sweet and sad voice and observing the gentle expression on her pale and melancholy face, she calmed down.

— Daughter of mortals! said the figure. Why do your tears disturb the waters of my fountain and your sighs interrupt the silence of the night?

— I am weeping for the falseness of men, and I am complaining about my loneliness.

—There is still a solution for your sorrows. Look at me, a Moorish princess who like you, was unlucky in love. A Christian knight who was your ancestor captivated my heart and proposed to take me to his land and to the heart of his faith. I had become a convert at heart, but I doubted and then it was too late. For that reason the evil spirits have me imprisoned and enchanted in this tower, until some Christian soul breaks the magic spell. Would you be prepared to do that?

...the fountain began bubbling up and the Moorish lady appeared again.

The young maiden, trembling, agreed to do so.

—Come close and do not be afraid. Dip your hand in the fountain and baptise me according to the rites of your religion. So the enchantment will be broken and my spirit will rest in peace.

So the maiden poured the water over the phantom. The figure gave a smile of incredible sweetness, laid her lute at Jacinta's feet, crossed her arms and disappeared into the fountain like a shower of dew.

The maiden left, astonished and full of fear. She could hardly sleep, but when day broke and she woke up, everything seemed like a nightmare. However, in the hall was the evidence of the reality of her dream: next to the fountain was the silver lute shining in the morning sun.

She ran in search of her aunt and told her what had happened, and all the doubts which her elderly relative might have had disappeared when her niece plucked the lute; such moving notes were heard that even Fredegunda's icy heart —a region of perpetual winter— melted. Only a supernatural melody could have produced such an effect.

The extraordinary power of the lute became more and more famous. Travellers stopped on their way, spellbound at the foot of the tower. The birds stopped chirping and singing to listen. The inhabitants of Granada climbed up to the Alhambra to hear the magical music that floated around the Tower of the Princesses.

The pretty young minstrel ventured out of her retreat. Rich and powerful people were eager for her attention, since the magical lute drew the highest society to their saloons. Her aunt was always there to accompany her, like a dragon that scared off her passionate admirers. Her name spread from one city to another; nothing was talked about in the whole of Andalusia except the minstrel of the Alhambra.

While Andalusia was humming with activity and interest in this magical music, other things were happening in the court of Philip V, an unfortunate and extravagant monarch full of strange whims. There were times when he was in bed for weeks, complaining of all types of imaginary illnesses. At other times he was intent on abandoning the throne, to the great annoyance of his wife, who enjoyed the glory of being queen and who, because of the monarch's weakness, ruled the country.

In fact, music turned out to be the most efficient remedy for the king's illness, therefore the queen surrounded herself with the best musicians and even summoned the famous Italian singer Farinelli.

About this time, the illustrious Bourbon monarch was overcome by a greater obsession than all his previous ones. After a period of imaginary illness, which defied all the musicians and their concerts, the monarch considered himself to be really dead.

This would have been harmless enough, and even fairly convenient, if he had been content to remain quiet, as is fitting to a dead person, but he insisted on having funeral rites performed, and became impatient because of the indolence or lack of respect of those who were leaving him unburied. But what could be done? To disobey the king's orders was very serious. But to obey him and bury him alive would be to commit regicide!

In the middle of this dilemma, the fame of a young artist admired throughout Andalusia reached the court and she was summoned to appear in San Ildefonso where the court resided.

A few days later, while the queen was walking in the gardens with her ladies in waiting, the lute-player was presented to her. Isabella was surprised by her noble and at the same time unpretending appearance, with her picturesque Andalusian dress, the silver instrument in her hands and her eyes with a downcast and modest look. Her beauty and elegance proclaimed her as the Rose of the Alhambra.

As always, she was accompanied by her vigilant aunt, Fredegunda, who informed the queen of the family history of her niece. Isabella was pleased to know that she was from an aristocratic family, although impoverished, and that her father had died fighting in the service of the crown.

—If you are able to banish the evil spirit that has taken possession of your sovereign, then I shall take care of your fortune and lavish honours and riches on you.

Impatiently she led her to the room of the capricious king, a huge room hung with black and the windows closed to avoid the daylight. The wax tapers gave a lugubrious light that dimly lit the mourning courtiers with their sad expressions. On his funeral bed, hands crossed on his chest and just the tip of his nose perceptible, lay the fictitious "dead man".

The beautiful lute player plucked her instrument nervously, but she soon calmed down and recovered her confidence as she played her melodies, which were so heavenly that they hardly seemed to be played by a human. The king, already considered to be in the world of spirits, thought it was heavenly music. The strong voice changed tone and putting her whole heart into it, she began a ballad that told a tale of the

Alhambra and the Moors. The king's gloomy heart was enchanted by the music and he immediately abandoned his bed.

The triumph of the magic flute was complete. His grief disappeared and it was as though a dead person had returned to life. The windows were opened, the rays of brilliant sunlight entered into the gloomy room and all eyes were in search of the enchanting singer; but the lute had slid out of her hand, she herself had fallen to the ground and a moment afterwards was lifted up in the arms of Ruíz de Alarcón.

Shortly afterwards there was a splendid celebration of the wedding and the Rose of the Alhambra became the delight of the court.

But the reader may well wonder, how did the page account to Jacinta for his long absence?

This is easy to explain: his absence was due to the opposition of his old and arrogant father. Besides, young people who love each other soon forget about past grievances when they meet up again.

So how did this proud old father allow the marriage?

A very simple matter: his scruples were soon dispelled when he saw the rewards that were showered on the royal favourite; besides, the magical powers of the lute were capable of overcoming even the most stubborn head.

So what happened to the enchanted lute?

That is a very curious thing and goes to show the truth of our story. For some time the lute remained in the family, but it was thought to have been stolen by the singer Farinelli, out of jealousy. On his death, it passed into other hands that were ignorant of its magical qualities, the silver was melted down and the strings used for an old Cremona violin. These strings still retain something of that magic; that violin, which fascinates the whole world, is the violin of Paganini!

The
Two Discreet
Statues

The Tower of Comares reflected in the Myrtle Court

The Two Discreet Statues

In one of the Alhambra rooms there used to live a man called Lope Sánchez, who worked in the gardens. He was a very merry and active fellow, the life and soul of the fortress, and when he finished his work he would sit on a bench and strum his guitar and sing ballads about heroic deeds to amuse the soldiers of the fortress, or merry boleros and fandangos for the young girls to dance to.

Like most little men, Lope Sánchez had a tall, robust wife, who could almost have fitted him in her pocket. However, instead of ten little children, as most poor people had, he only had one daughter of twelve, a small and black-eyed girl who was as merry as him. She was called Sanchica and was the delight of his heart; she played beside him as he worked in the gardens, danced to the rhythm of his guitar and ran like a young fawn through the woods, groves and ruined palace halls.

It was the eve of the festivity of St. John and at night the people of the Alhambra climbed up to the Mountain of the Sun, high above the Generalife, to celebrate there. It was a clear night and the moonlight shone on the mountains and left the city, with its domes and spires, bathed in shade, and the valley looked like fairyland, with its streams shining like silver bands. High on the top of the mountain they lit a bonfire, according to the customs handed down from Moorish times. The inhabitants of the nearby countryside celebrated this night too and lit bonfires in different parts of the valley and on the mountainside.

The evening passed by gaily, with dancing to the guitar of Lope Sánchez. During the dancing, Sanchica was playing with her little friends among the ruins of the old Moorish fort on the town of the mountain, when she found a little hand carved in black jet, with the fingers closed and the thumb closely clutched over them. She showed her mother her discovery, and it immediately became the subject of commentaries and superstitious doubts.

—Throw it away!

—It's Moorish and may be spellbound.

—You can sell it in the Zacatín.

An old soldier who had served in Africa examined the hand with a very knowing look.

—I have seen things like this in Barbary, he said. This is a lucky talisman against the evil eye and spells. I congratulate you, my friend Lope, this will bring good luck to your daughter.

On hearing this, her mother hung the little jet hand on a ribbon around her daughter's neck.

The talisman reminded people of the stories and superstitions about the Moors. The dancing was forgotten and they sat on the ground telling old legends of their ancestors. Some of the tales were about the wonders of the mountain where they were at that moment, both a famous mountain and a place of fantasy. One old lady gave a detailed description of the underground palace below the hill, where Boabdil and his Muslim court are said to be enchanted.

—Among those ruins, she said, pointing to some tumbled-down walls in the distance, there is a deep well that reaches right down to the heart of the mountain. Many moons ago, a poor man who kept his goats on this mountain went down in search of a kid that had fallen in. He came out pale with fear, telling such tales that everyone thought he had gone mad. He spent a couple of days raving about the Moorish ghosts that had pursued him in the cave, and it was hard to persuade him to return to the mountain with his goats. When he finally did so, he was never seen again. His goats were found wandering among the ruins and his hat and cloak beside the well, but no one ever knew what happened to him.

Sanchica listened to the story with great curiosity and was very eager to peep into the pit. She crept away from her companions, searched for the ruins and felt her way towards a little hollow that sloped down to the valley of the Darro. In the centre of this hollow was the well, and the young girl approached the edge and peeped down. The bottom was pitch-black and she stepped back, frightened; then she looked again and stepped back once more; she peeped in a third time, because the fear rather thrilled her. Finally, she threw in a stone that fell noiselessly for some time; then she heard it strike against the side, bouncing from one side to the other, tumbling with a noise like thunder, until it finally fell into the water far below and all was silent once more.

But not for long. It seemed as though something

had woken up in this terrible abyss. A buzzing sound gradually rose out of the pit; it grew louder and sounded like a confusion of voices, the clash of arms and the sound of trumpets, as though an army was preparing for combat in the depths of the earth.

Sanchica ran away in silent terror, in search of her parents and companions, but they had all left and only the smouldering remains of the bonfire could be seen in the moonlight. The distant bonfires on the mountains and in the valley had all extinguished too and silence reigned. She shouted out, but there was no reply. The little girl rushed down the mountainside and through the gardens of the Generalife to the alley of trees leading to the Alhambra, where she sat to recover her breath. The bell on the watchtower tolled midnight. Silence reigned everywhere, nature seemed to be asleep except for the gentle trickling of a stream under the bushes. She was almost falling asleep, when she caught sight of something shining in the distance in the moonlight, and realised it was a long cavalcade of Moorish soldiers marching down the mountain through the wooded avenues. They were armed with lances, shields, scimitars, axes and clad in armour; they were mounted on horseback, but their hoofs were noiseless, as though they were shod with felt. Among the horsemen, all as pale as death, there was a beautiful lady, wearing a crown on her head and long, golden locks entwined with pearls. Her horse's trappings were of crimson velvet and reached down to the ground. She looked disconsolate and her eyes were downcast.

Behind them came a train of courtiers, with elegant robes and turbans and in the middle of them, on horseback, was King Boabdil el Chico, with a cape covered in jewels and a crown of diamonds. Sanchica recognised him from the portrait she had seen in the art gallery in the Generalife. She watched the royal procession in amazement, and although she knew it was something magical and enchanted, she watched it armed with the courage she had from the little hand that hung from her neck.

Then she stood up and followed the cavalcade that continued towards the Gate of Justice that was wide open to receive it. The old invalid soldiers lay on the stone benches buried in a magical dream, and the escort passed beside them noiselessly and with the banners flying in triumph. The young girl would have liked to follow behind them, but she noticed an opening in the earth that led to the foundations of the entrance tower. She went down some steps cut out of the rock and continuing through a passageway lit by silver perfumed lamps, she reached a great hall opened up in the heart of the mountain, magnificently furnished. Lying back on a divan sat an old man with a white beard, dressed in Moorish style, nodding away and holding a stick that seemed to be slipping out of his grasp. Very near him was a beautiful woman dressed in old Spanish dress and wearing a crown of diamonds and pearls, and playing softly on a silver lyre. Sanchica then remembered a certain story of a Christian princess imprisoned in the centre of the mountain by an Arab astrologer, whom she in turn kept spellbound thanks to the power of music.

The lady was surprised to see a mortal in the enchanted hall.

—Is it the eve of St. John? she asked.

—Yes, it is, replied the young girl.

—Then my magic charm is temporarily in suspension. I am a Christian, like you, although I am a prisoner here because of a spell. Touch my chains with the talisman you have around your neck and I shall be free for this night.

As she said this, she showed a broad golden band around her waist and a golden chain that held her fastened to the ground. The young girl held the hand of jet next to the golden band and the chain fell loose.

The noise woke the old man, but the princess struck the chords of the lyre and he fell back into his sleep.

—Now touch his stick with the talisman!

The young girl did just this and the stick slipped out of the hand of the astrologer, who fell into the deepest sleep. The lady held the silver lyre on the divan near the old man's head and struck the chords again.

Oh spirit of harmony! she said, chain up his senses until the next day dawns. Now, follow me, my child, she continued, and you will see what the Alhambra was like in its period of glory, because your talisman can reveal all its marvels.

They went up through the entry to the cavern to the Gate of Justice and reached the *Plaza de los Aljibes*, the esplanade inside the fortress. It was full of squadrons of Moorish soldiers, both infantry and cavalry, royal guards and rows of black African soldiers with their swords drawn. In the middle of a deathly silence, the brave little girl followed behind her guide. Her astonishment grew as she entered the palace where she had been brought up: the full moon lit up the halls, courts and gardens as though it were daylight, but there was a completely different air to the whole scene. The walls no longer seemed stained or cracked and they were covered with rich silks from Damascus instead of cobwebs; the gilt and the arabesque paintings shone with their original brilliance. The halls were no longer empty, but were furnished with ottomans and sofas covered with pearls and precious stones, and the fountains were playing in the courts and gardens.

The kitchens were a hive of activity: the cooks were busy preparing exotic dishes, roasting the phantoms of chicken and partridges, while servants were rushing here and there with great dishes of food. The Court of Lions was full of the activity of guards, courtiers and Muslim experts in religious law, just as it was in Moorish times. In the Hall of Judgement sat Boabdil on his throne, surrounded by his court and brandishing his sceptre. In spite of all this throng of people and the corresponding bustle, there was not a sound to be heard in the midnight silence, except for the trickle of the fountains. Sanchica was speechless in amazement and followed the princess right through the palace until they reached the doorway to the vaulted passages underneath the Tower of Comares. On either side of the door was a statue of a nymph in white marble; their heads were turned towards the inside of the vault.

—These statues guard a treasure hidden by a Mus-

Tell your father to search in the direction where their eyes are looking and he will become the richest man in Granada...

lim king in the old days. Tell your father to search the spot where their eyes are staring and he will become the richest man in Granada. But thanks to the talisman, you are the only person who will be able to take the treasure. Advise him to use it wisely and to devote part of it for daily masses that will free me from this enchantment.

Then the lady took the little girl to the Garden of Lindaraxa, next to the vault of the statues. The moon trembled on the waters of a solitary fountain and shone its tenuous light on the orange and lemon trees. The beautiful lady crowned Sanchica's head with a wreath made from a branch of myrtle.

This will remind you of what I have revealed to you. The time for my return has come. Do not follow me, do not forget my words, and have masses said for my freedom.

So she entered into the passageways under the Tower of Comares and was never seen again.

A cock crowed in the distance and a pale light began to appear over the eastern mountains; a breeze blew and a sound rather like dry leaves rustled through the courtyards and corridors and all the doors creaked and closed with a bang.

Sanchica returned to the scenes filled by the crowds

of people before, but Boabdil and his court had disappeared. The moon shone on the halls and galleries be-
reft of their short-lived splendour, now hung with cobwebs once again. The only sounds were the flitting of
the bat and the croaking of the frogs.

So the little girl made her way towards her family's
modest home, where the door was always open, since
Lope Sánchez was too poor to need locks or bolts. She
tiptoed to her little bed, placed the myrtle wreath under the pillow and soon fell asleep.

In the morning she told her father all that had happened, but he imagined it was a dream and marched
off to his work in the garden, but soon afterwards he
saw his little daughter running breathlessly towards
him.

—Father! she cried. Look at the myrtle wreath the
Moorish lady put on my head!

Lope was astonished; the stalk was of pure gold and
each leaf a shining emerald! He was not used to precious stones, but he knew enough to realise that this
was something far more substantial than what dreams
are made of, and that at least his daughter had dreamt
profitably. The first thing he did was to tell Sanchica
to keep it all a secret. Then he went in search of the
vault of the nymphs, and there they were, sure enough,

both looking towards the same place inside the building; he marvelled at the ingenious way of guarding the secret; he made a mark on the point in the wall where the nymphs were looking, then he left.

Lope was nervous all day long. He wandered about near the statues, worried that someone should discover everything. He trembled at every footstep he heard. He would have liked to turn their heads in another direction, but he did not take into account the fact that they had been looking there for centuries without anyone noticing it.

"A plague on them! he would say to himself, they are going to discover everything. Has such a way of keeping a secret every been seen?"

If anyone approached, he would creep away furtively for fear of arousing any suspicions, then he returned to make sure, but he burst out angrily at the statues.

"Always looking, he thought to himself, looking exactly where they should not be. To hell with them! Just like all of their sex: if they do not have tongues to gossip with, they will do it with their eyes."

At length this long and anxious day came to an end. Lope Sánchez waited until the dead of night before venturing with his daughter into the hall where the two nymphs watched mysteriously over the hiding-place.

—With your permission, gentle ladies, I am going to relieve you of your guard of the last two or three centuries, which must have been very tiresome. At once he set to work on the sign on the wall and soon discovered a hole where there were two great porcelain jars, which he could not take out until his daughter touched them. With her help he took them out of the niche and to his great joy he found them full of Moorish gold coins, jewels and precious stones. Before dawn he took them to his room and left the two guardian statues still staring at the empty wall.

So this was how Lope Sánchez suddenly became rich; but his riches, as always happens, brought him a world of problems which he had never before known. How could he keep his treasure safely and enjoy it without arousing suspicions? For the first time in his life he was afraid of robbers and he set to work barricading the doors and windows, but even so he could not sleep in peace. He lost his good sense of humour, he no longer joked nor sang with the neighbours and he became the most miserable creature in the Alhambra. His old friends began to turn their backs on him, thinking that he must be in need and afraid that he would ask for their help. Little did they know that his only misfortune was his riches!

Lope's wife used to go to her confessor, Fray Simón, for advice. He was a stout Franciscan friar who was the spiritual comfort of half the women in the neighbourhood. He was also very well respected by the different sisterhoods of nuns, who rewarded his services with sweet biscuits and liquors from their convents, for his enjoyment after fasts and vigils.

Fray Simón thrived carrying out his functions but, in spite of his healthy look, a knotted rope tied around his waist proved his austerity. People took off their hats to that mirror of piety and even the dogs perceived his scent of saintliness and barked from their kennels.

So this was the spiritual counsellor of Lope's wife, who was soon informed with great mystery about everything.

—Daughter of my soul! exclaimed the friar crossing himself. Your husband has committed a double crime! Treasure found in royal domains belongs to the crown, but since it is the wealth of infidels, snatched from Satan, it should be devoted to the church. However, we shall see how we can reach an agreement. Bring me the myrtle wreath.

When the good friar saw it, his eyes sparkled at the size and beauty of the emeralds.

—I will hang this up as an offering before the image of San Francisco, he said, and I will pray to him to allow your husband to enjoy your wealth in peace.

The good woman was happy to make her peace with heaven at such a cheap price, and the friar took the wreath to his convent with saintly steps.

When Lope returned home and discovered what had happened he was very annoyed, since he did not have his wife's devotion, nor did he approve of the friar's visits.

—What have you done? he said. You have put everything in danger with your gossiping.

—What? Are you going to forbid me from confessing?

—No, you can confess as many of your sins as you like, but that treasure is my sin, and my conscience is at ease under the weight of it.

It was useless to complain. Once the secret was discovered, the only hope was to trust in Friar Simon's discretion. The next day he returned.

—Daughter, he said, San Francisco appeared to me in my dreams last night, and he spoke to my angrily: "How can you dare to pray to me to renounce the treasure of the Gentiles, knowing the poverty of my chapel? In my name, ask Lope Sánchez for part of the gold to make two candlesticks, and let him enjoy the rest.

Lope's wife crossed herself in fear, filled a large purse with pieces of Moorish gold and handed it over to the friar. He in turn gave her so many blessings that if Heaven were to pay them, they would enrich even the last generation.

When Lope discovered this second donation, he nearly lost his senses and his wife calmed him down with difficulty, reminding him of the immense riches he still had and how little had been donated to San Francisco.

However, Friar Simón kept many needy relations and half a dozen orphans under his care, so he repeated his visits with petitions for Saint Dominic, Saint Andrew and Saint James. Lope was in despair, and he realised that unless he was out of the reach of the friar he would have to make donations to all the saints in the calendar. Therefore he decided to escape in secret to another part of the kingdom with the remains of the treasure.

He bought a strong mule with this in mind, and he hid it under the Tower of the Seven Floors, where it was said that Velludo, a phantom headless horse, came

Too late, he realised that he was riding the terrible Velludo!

out at night and ran around the streets of Granada followed by a pack of hell-hounds. Lope Sánchez did not believe in that story, but he imagined that nobody would dare to venture into the stable of the phantom horse. He sent his family to a distant village in the Vega and, late at night, he took his treasure to the tower, loaded it on to the mule and led it cautiously down the dark avenue.

Honest Lope had mentioned nothing of this to anyone, except to his faithful wife, but due no doubt to some miraculous revelation, Friar Simón knew about it. He realised that the infidel riches were about to be lost from his clutches so he decided on another attack for the benefit of the church and San Francisco. When the bell rang for *ánimas* and all the Alhambra was silent, he hid among the roses and laurels along the avenue. He stayed there, counting the quarter hours and listening to the owls hooting and the distant barking of dogs in the gypsy caves.

He finally heard the sound of hoofs and in the darkness he vaguely distinguished a horse coming down the avenue. Rejoicing at the trick he was going to play on Lope, the friar tucked up his long skirts and waited until his prey was in front of him and leapt straight on to the horse.

—Ah ha! Now we shall see who understands the game, exclaimed the stout friar.

Hardly had he spoken these words when the mule began to kick, rear and gallop downhill at full speed. The friar tried to halt him, but in vain; the friar's habit was torn, his shaven head was scratched from the brambles and knocked by the branches and with horror he saw a pack of seven hounds racing behind him. Too late, he realised that he was riding the terrible Velludo!

Down the avenue, across Plaza Nueva, along the Zacatín and Bibarrambla, in a fiendish race and an infernal disturbance. The friar was invoking all the saints and the Holy Virgin, but it seemed that every saint's name he mentioned was like the prick of the spurs and Velludo jumped as high as a house. Against his will, Friar Simón was carried here and there all night long, until all his bones ached and a particular part of his body became almost skinless.

Finally, with the cock's crow, the phantom-like horse returned in the direction of its tower. Across Bibarrambla, through the Zacatín, Plaza Nueva and the grove. The seven dogs dropped back howling, barking and on the heels of the terrified friar. As it arrived at its retreat, the phantom horse kicked up its heels and threw the friar through the air, disappeared inside the dark vault and silence reigned.

Has such a diabolical trick ever been played on a holy friar? A farmworker found the unfortunate Friar Simón lying at the foot of the tower, so bruised and beaten about that he could neither speak nor move. He was taken to his cell and the rumour spread that he had been attacked by robbers. It took a couple of days before he recovered the use of his legs; in the meantime he consoled himself remembering the infidel riches he had laid his hands on before. As soon as he could move again he went in search of the crown and the gold he achieved through the piety of the wife of Lope Sanchez. To his amazement, he found nothing more than a branch of dried myrtle and some bags of sand and pebbles!

In spite of his anger, the friar had the good sense not to give his secret away, as people might make fun of him, and his superior might punish him. Only on his death-bed did he tell the story to his confessor of his night ride on the Velludo.

Lope Sánchez disappeared from the Alhambra and nothing was heard of him for a long time. Several years later, one of his old companions, an invalid soldier who was in Malaga, was run over by a coach drawn by six horses. An elderly, well-dressed gentleman with a wig and a sword, stepped down to help him, and the soldier recognised his old friend Lope, who was about to celebrate the wedding of his daughter Sanchica with a nobleman from the land. Inside the carriage was the wife of Sánchez, as plump as a barrel and covered in feathers, jewels, pearls, necklaces and rings. Sanchica had grown into a gracious and beautiful woman who looked like a duchess or even a princess. Sitting next to her was a rather withered little man who was thin, which proved his true blood; he was a real Spanish nobleman, who was hardly three cubits tall.

Lope took the invalid with him for several days and treated him like a king. He invited him to the theatre and to bullfights and gave him a farewell bag of money, one for him and another for his other companions in the Alhambra.

The discreet statues still stand there with their eyes staring significantly at the same place in the wall, which leads many people to suppose that there is still some treasure hidden away. Others, particularly the female visitors, contemplate the statues with the greatest pleasure, as lasting proof that women know how to keep secrets.

The Enchanted Soldier

View of the Alhambra from the Valley of the River Darro

The Enchanted Soldier

Many years ago there was a student from Salamanca called *Don* Vincent; he was one of those students who used to go around the villages and towns in their holidays, asking for money to allow them to continue studying another year. As he was keen on music, he took his guitar to amuse the villagers and to pay for his board and lodging.

Before setting out on his trips, he went to the square of the Carvajal Seminary and said a prayer to St Ciprian to ask for good luck, and when he lowered his eyes to the ground he saw a gold and silver ring, with a seal formed by two triangles crossed like a star. This is said to be a magic sign of great power, invented by the wise King Solomon, although Vincent was not aware of this. He slipped it on to his finger, considering it a reward from St. Ciprian for his prayer, then he set out happily on his way.

In Spain, a student without means travels as he wishes from village to village and from town to town. The parish priests, most of whom had also been poor students, give them board and lodging and even a few coins. Many educated men began their studies in this way. *Don* Vincent was a good-looking young man and a cheerful guitar-player, so he was always well received by the country folk, their wives and their children.

The young fellow travelled over half the country with the purpose of visiting the famous city of Granada. Sometimes he slept in the priest's house and other times in the modest home of a farm worker. He would sit by the door and play fandangos and boleros for the young girls and boys to dance to at dusk. In the morning his hosts' kind words and the gentle glance of their daughter would bid him farewell.

When he reached Granada, the aim of his musical travels, he was delighted to see the Moorish towers, the valley, the snowy mountains shining in the summer heat. He was full of curiosity; he peeped through doorways, walked around all the streets and gazed at the monuments. Any feminine face at a window seemed to him like a Zoraida or a Zelinda, any elegant lady seemed to be a Muslim princess.

He soon became popular in the old Moorish capital and its surroundings. Sometimes he would go to the Avellano fountain in the valley of the river Darro, which had been a popular meeting-place since the time of the Moors, and there he continued his studies of female beauty, a pastime he was particularly inclined to. In this delightful setting he would improvise love songs on his guitar, admiring the young folk or encouraging them to dance.

One afternoon he saw a priest arriving, and everybody took their hats off to him. He was the image of healthy life, though maybe not saintly, robust and red-faced; he arrived hot and sweating, handing out offerings in a charitable way, while everybody praised him. He walked up the hill, leaning on the arm of a young maid, an Andalusian damsel from top to toe, healthy and ardent in her gestures and movements, but at the same time so shy and discreet that if she looked at someone out of the corner of her eye she immediately looked down.

The priest sat on a stone bench in the middle of his audience and the maid took him a glass of cool, clear water, which he drank together with a sweetmeat.

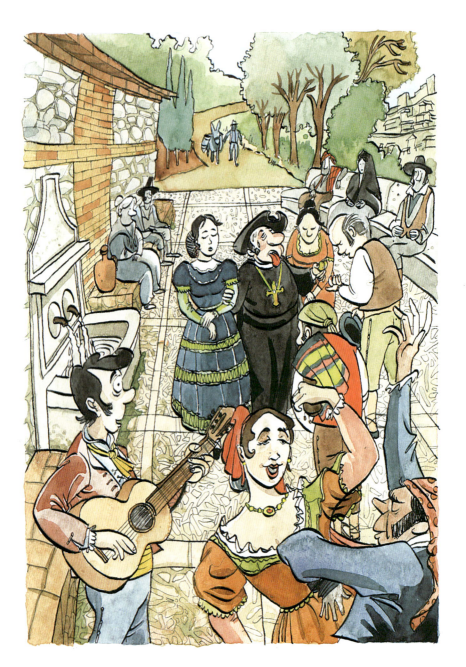

One afternoon he saw a priest arriving...

—How delightful, the student thought, to have such a charming little lamb for a companion!

But in vain the student tried out his approaches that were so successful with the priests and the young girls in the villages. He played his guitar and sang more movingly than ever, but the priest was no enthusiast of music and the young maid did not lift her eyes from the ground. They stayed a while by the fountain, and when they were leaving, the young girl gave the student a look that captivated his heart.

After they had left, he asked about them. Father Thomas was a pious and methodical priest: he would get up, go for a walk to give him an appetite, have lunch, sleep a siesta, play cards, have supper and retire to bed to regain strength to carry out the same obligations the next day. A housekeeper, who was an excellent cook, and the maid, lived with him.

That put an end to the happy and carefree life of the student! He spent day and night thinking about the young girl. He discovered his house, but a globetrotter like him was not well received by the priest, who had never been a needy student obliged to sing for his living. During the day, Vincent waited for the young maid to come to the window, but her expression only fanned his passion without giving him any hopes. He also sang her nightly serenades, and once his hopes were raised on seeing something white approach the window, but it was only the priest's night-cap! The poor student was in despair.

The eve of St. John arrived, when the people of Granada go out into the countryside and dance all the evening and all night long by the Darro and the Genil rivers. Those who wash their face in the river as the cathedral clock strikes twelve will be lucky, because at that moment the river water has magical beautify-ing powers.

Don Vincent also went along to the valley of the Darro, under the Alhambra hill and towers. Many groups of people danced under the vines and the fig trees, to the sound of guitars and castanets.

The student leant sadly against the end of a bridge, watching the happy couples and feeling bitterly sorry for himself in his sadness and poverty.

Gradually his attention was attracted by a tall, rough-looking soldier with a grey beard, who stood motionless as though on guard at the other end of the bridge. He wore a Spanish suit of armour, shield and lance, but in spite of his strange aspect, he went un-noticed by those who were crossing the river next to him.

– You are wearing a strange old suit of armour, my friend, said the student, approaching him.

–I belong to the escort of Ferdinand and Isabella, grunted the soldier in a gruff voice. I have been standing guard here for three centuries, and I trust that one day my turn will come. If you have both faith and courage, follow me, and you will make a fortune.

–I have nothing to lose, except my life and an old guitar, neither of them of much value. But if I have to commit some crime to improve my luck, I prefer to remain poor.

–I am an old Christian, answered the soldier, offended. – Trust me and do not be afraid.

Our student followed him with admiration. He observed that people stepped aside for his companion as though he were invisible. He crossed the bridge, passed by a mill and a Moorish aqueduct, climbed up the steep cliff separating the Generalife from the Alhambra and arrived, almost at night time, at the foot of a deserted and ruinous tower. The soldier knocked on the foundations with his lance and the stones opened up silently, revealing a great entranceway.

The young student shivered, but made the sign of the cross, whispered a hail Mary and followed his mysterious guide to a deep vault in the rock underneath the tower and covered with Arabic lettering.

—This has been my bed since three hundred years ago.

—Blessed St. Anthony! exclaimed Vincent. What heavy sleep you must have had, just like the hardness of your bed.

— To the contrary, I have been constantly awake, replied the soldier. I was taken prisoner in an attack against the Moors and shut up in this tower. When the fortress was about to be handed over to the Catholic Monarchs, I helped a Muslim priest to hide some of Boabdil's treasures here and was punished for my deed. The priest put a spell on me so that I would guard his treasures, but he never returned, so since then I have been buried alive. On the night of St. John once every one hundred years, the spell is broken, and I can go to the bridge where you saw me, until somebody breaks the spell. Until now, this all of this has proved useless, because no living beings have been able to see me. You are the first one who has spoken to me, thanks to the talisman of Solomon's ring, and I depend on you to free me from this imprisonment or leave me to continue keeping guard for another hundred years.

The student listened to the tale in amazement. He had heard plenty of stories about enchanted treasures in the Alhambra, but he had never believed them. In spite of the power of the charm, it was intimidating to find himself face to face in such a place with a spell-bound soldier who should have been peacefully in his grave three hundred years ago.

Such a person could not be made fun of, so the young man promised him his friendship and his desire to free him. Then the soldier showed him a little locked iron chest.

—This coffer, he said, contains gold, jewels and precious stones. Destroy the spell that binds me and half of this wealth will be yours.

—But what must I do?

—You need a priest who will banish the evil spirits and a young Christian girl who will touch the coffer with Solomon's seal. But the priest must be a model of saintliness and must fast for twenty-four hours before coming here, and the young girl must be chaste and innocent. You must hurry to find them, because my permission finishes in three days' time; if by then I have not been freed, I shall have to keep guard for another century.

—I know both the priest and the young girl you have described, said the student. But how shall I enter the tower again?

—The seal will open it for you.

Our hero left happily and the wall closed behind him.

The next morning he made his way towards the house of Father Thomas, this time not as a vagrant musician, but as the bearer of a world of magical treasures. We do not know what they talked about, but the priest was full of enthusiasm about the idea of freeing the soldier and the coffer from the hands of Satan. How many offerings could be given to the poor, how many churches could be built, how many poor relatives could be enriched!

The young maiden was also willing to help.

The difficult part was the fast: twice the good priest tried it, without success. The third day he felt stronger in the face of the temptations of his larder, but it was necessary to prove that he could resist until the spell was broken.

Late at night they set out towards the deep valley, carrying a lantern and a basket of food to banish the demon of hunger as soon as the other spirits had been banished.

Solomon's seal opened the tower for them, and there was the soldier awaiting their arrival, sitting on the chest. The spell was cast, the young maiden touched the locks with the ring, the lid burst open and there was the treasure of gold and jewels, almost dazzling their eyes!

— Quickly, let's go! cried the student, full of joy, filling his pockets.

—Slowly! said the soldier. Let's take out the coffer and divide up the riches.

They began to do this,with difficulty, because the chest was heavy. While they wrestled with it, the priest went to one side and launched his attack against the spectre of hunger that rumbled inside him; in no time he devoured a chicken together with a big swig of wine...

Breaking his fast had a disastrous effect: the soldier gave a cry of despair; the half-opened coffer moved back to its place and closed again. The priest, student and young maiden found themselves outside the tower, whose walls closed with a crash.

Vincent wanted to go in again, but the frightened young maiden had dropped Solomon's seal inside the vault.

The cathedral bells struck twelve, the spell commenced once more and the poor soldier began his guard duty for another hundred years, locked in with his treasure, while these three sad people wandered forlornly down the valley.

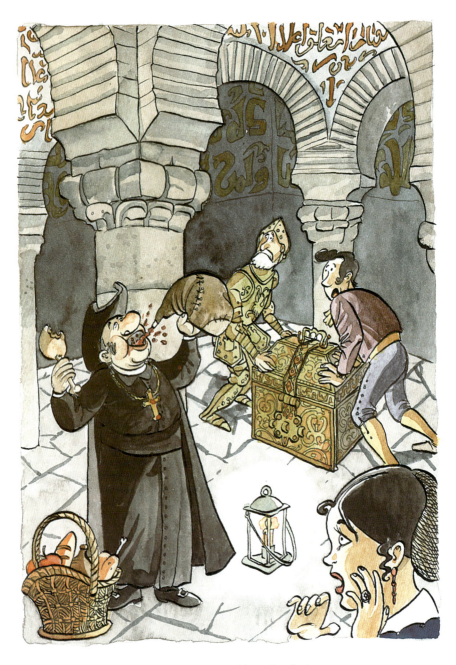

...in no time he devoured a chicken with a big swig of wine...

And so the legend reaches its end, as far as we have been able to prove. Tradition says that the student had enough riches in his pocket to improve his situation, and he became a prosperous man, so the priest allowed him to marry the young maiden, who gave her husband a large family.

People say that the soldier in still on guard on the Darro bridge on the night of St. John, and he is still invisible, except to those lucky people who possess Solomon's seal.